Copyright © 2017 by Dan Jenkins.
All rights reserved.
This book, or parts thereof, may not be reproduced in any form without permission
from the publisher; exceptions are made for brief excerpts used in published reviews.

Published by
TYRUS BOOKS
an imprint of F+W Media, Inc.
10151 Carver Road, Suite 200
Blue Ash, OH 45242. U.S.A.
www.tyrusbooks.com

Hardcover ISBN 10: 1-5072-0147-8
Hardcover ISBN 13: 978-1-5072-0147-3
Paperback ISBN 10: 1-5072-0146-X
Paperback ISBN 13: 978-1-5072-0146-6
eISBN 10: 1-5072-0148-6
eISBN 13: 978-1-5072-0148-0

Printed in the United States of America.

10 9 8 7 6 5 4 3 2 1

Library of Congress Cataloging-in-Publication Data
Jenkins, Dan, author.
Stick a fork in me / Dan Jenkins.
Blue Ash, OH: Tyrus Books, 2017.
CCN 2016040608 | ISBN 9781507201473 (hc) | ISBN 1507201478 (hc) | ISBN
507201466 (pb) | ISBN 150720146X (pb) | ISBN 9781507201480 (ebook) | ISBN
1507201486 (ebook)
Sports stories. | BISAC: FICTION / Humorous. | FICTION / Sports. | GSAFD:
Humorous fiction.
LCC PS3560.E48 S75 2017 | DDC 813/.54--dc23
LC record available at https://lccn.loc.gov/2016040608

a work of fiction. Names, characters, corporations, institutions, organizations,
or locales in this novel are either the product of the author's imagination or,
used fictitiously. The resemblance of any character to actual persons (living or
entirely coincidental.

f the designations used by manufacturers and sellers to distinguish their
are claimed as trademarks. Where those designations appear in this book
Media, Inc., was aware of a trademark claim, the designations have been
with initial capital letters.

Cover design by Erin Alexander.
images © wiml/Agnieszka Murphy/Anna Kudinova/Oleg Labunets/123RF.

This book is available at quantity discounts for bulk purchases.
For information, please call 1-800-289-0963.

STICK A FORK IN ME

A NOVEL

DAN JENKINS

L
9781

LCSH

This is
events,
if real,
dead) i

Many
product
and F+V
printed

Cover

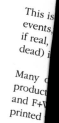

TYRUS
BOOKS

For Sally, Marty, and Danny,
*my daughter and two sons who make me proud every day,
with love and thanks for your contributions to this effort,
some of it unknowingly, of course.*

EPIGRAPH

"Fortunately, there's still a large segment of young men and women in America who go to college for the right reasons—to get drunk, get laid, and root for the football team."

—Pete Wallace, Athletic Director, Western Ohio University.

ONE

WHEN I took this athletic director's job fifteen years ago I knew the toughest part would be trying to keep our football scholars eligible so they could make the Big U. prouder and richer with their jitterbugging touchdown scampers. This meant sucking up to the left-loon professors in the Political Science building. I do believe those sumbitches would like to give America away to a bunch of goat-herders, or some other pack of off-brand foreigners who dress silly. It meant being nice to the bleeding hearts in the Human Rights compound so they wouldn't call me a racist if they saw me eating a Ding Dong in public. And it meant there'd be times when I'd need to send a young stud on my staff over to the Journalism department to do a little public relations work, or, as he liked to put it, calling on his knowledge of Elizabethan language, "You mean go over there and duty-fuck the literary nympho chicks."

I'm sitting here reminiscing, is all.

Me. Pete Wallace. The most persevering, glad-handing AD who ever worked in higher education. I have a voice recorder going, but whatever I say will be for my ears only. I want to preserve a bunch of fond and not-so-fond memories for the book I may write someday on what it's like backstage in the world of big-time college sports.

I'd start the book off on the day four months ago when I was in my office waiting for the Board of Trustees to act on my voluntary retirement compensation. I was hoping the trustees were going to make me rich enough to buy my wife Glenda the winter home she liked in Cabo and the summer home she liked in Aspen. We never should have visited those places.

Personally, all I wanted was for the board to come up with a good-enough package to help me pay off the taxes and upkeep on our cozy English cottage here in University Gardens. That, and help us afford our dues and bills at Bent Oak Country Club. I thought Glenda ought to be happy knowing she could keep on playing golf and gin and poker with her lady friends at the club.

Glenda believed the Big U. always low-balled me on my salary. Even after I'd be given a raise, she'd say, "You can stick a fork in yourself—you're done."

I was looking forward to retirement. Eating at normal hours. Reading a good book instead of a balance sheet. Maybe taking one of those river cruises to see if Europe is still Europe or going by another name now. And not having to crawl out of bed at four in the morning to bail a moron out of jail, like a big defensive end who's been arrested on a charge of domestic violence.

This happened too often over the years. It worked a mental hardship on me and our football coach, Talk Big Taggert. It gave Talk Big a throbbing headache to weigh the importance of a strong pass rush against his strict rule of "zero tolerance" for domestic violence.

Coach Taggert liked his name of "Talk Big." I suppose I'd like it myself if I'd been born Taylor Taggert and seen it shortened to Tay as a kid. He recalled that it wasn't easy to meet somebody and say, "Hi, I'm Tay Taggert," without sounding like he had a lisp.

He was a graduate of the Big U., which is how most of us refer to Western Ohio University, a private institution in Shackayooka, Ohio, on the banks of the Shackayooka River, founded in 1852, enrollment 26,700 undergrad.

Talk Big was an option quarterback and earned his nickname as a sophomore starter. It was strapped on by a Pitt linebacker on his first possession in the opening game.

His voice could easily be heard anywhere. I even heard it standing on the sideline in my suit and tie when he called out, "Brown right foxtrot D-arrow Chicago 73 X-curl on three—break!"

When he moved to the line of scrimmage the Pitt linebacker grinned at him and said, "We could hear you, kid. What do they call you, Talk Big?"

His teammates fell about laughing, got a delay of game penalty, and the name stuck to him like money on a politician's palm.

Talk Big is a sayings and slogans man. The dressing room is covered up with inspirational messages, like this one from Hall of Fame coach Lou Holtz:

> A player who complains about the way the football
> bounces is probably the guy who dropped it.

And this one from the Dallas Cowboys' Emmitt Smith, while he was juggling three Super Bowl rings:

> Winning at football doesn't happen when the crowd roars.
> It happens every day when you prepare mentally and
> physically, and every night when you dream.

■ ■ ■

THERE WERE two decent humans on the fourteen-member board that I felt I could count on when it came to looking out for my interests, even though they were outnumbered by troublesome bobbleheads.

One of my moles was the chairman of the board, Roy Clapper. Roy runs a bank in town that his granddaddy started. Roy's an asshole who works at it, but he was *my* asshole. He helped me accomplish things in my job, and kept the bobbleheads under control. One of the bobbleheads only cared about the department of Performing Arts. Another one only cared about "inclusiveness."

Roy Clapper had to step on their necks now and then. Roy's in his early fifties and he'd been chairman of the trustees for twenty years. He terrorized the bobbleheads into voting "No" on anything that didn't involve somebody giving money to the university.

I'll put it this way. If an old Nazi war criminal emerged from the Brazilian jungle and wanted to donate $30 million to the university to further the studies of *wienerschnitzel* as body armor, Roy Clapper would grab his money in a heartbeat, slice off a finder's fee for himself, and order a bronze statue of the former Berlin resident erected in the middle of the Quad.

But that wouldn't make the Big U. different from any other top-drawer school today. I feel for parents these days who have to scrape up $60,000 a year for a kid's tuition. After four years the kid will be lucky if he or she missed all the lectures on what a fun-loving guy Karl Marx was. And luckier still if they don't graduate admiring radical terrorists for their courage and ridiculing Christians for their faith. When I become dictator, it'll be a felony for tenured professors to hide behind "academic freedom" and teach that claptrap.

I tried to avoid political discussions with our profs. The discussions usually ended up with me telling one of them he ought to be thankful he won the birth lottery and was a United States citizen, but he was welcome to go live in a third-world shithole and get back to me on how much fun it is.

In my time here I presided over an athletic budget that grew from $76 million a year to $102 million, with 40 percent of it going for football.

At any major university football is the straw that stirs the drink. Which means that every so often you have to remind the educators that 80,000 people never fill a stadium to watch a math quiz.

Fortunately, there's still a large segment of young men and women in America today who go to college for the right reasons—to get drunk, get laid, and root for the football team.

The winning football program during my reign increased our number of staunch donors by the hundreds, and quadrupled the number of applications from students who want to enter the world of what universities call "higher learning" and families call "bankruptcy."

Our faculty is loaded with bookish little men in beards, guys nourishing their ponytails, and women trying to look like Buffy Sainte-Marie. They believe kids come here for our diversified test tubes, multicultural coffee breaks, and a yearning to speak Somali. But as I've said, I had to get along with the profs as best I could, so I patted them on the head, treated them to steak dinners, and slipped bowl-game rings on their fingers.

■ ■ ■

MY OFFICE was in the hoops dome, or I should say, the Roy Clapper Coliseum. The mandatory treasures were on display. Game balls. Plaques. Photos of me with people who used to be somebody.

The football coaches and the sports information office are in a relatively new area built above the stadium's south end zone seats. Their elevator and escalator didn't come cheap. The coaches of other sports were in the Athletics building next door to the coliseum.

My office had sliding glass doors that opened onto a patio with tables, chairs, and umbrellas where I entertained when it was warm and looked at snow when it wasn't. I had a wet bar, a fridge, and a Cuisinart coffee maker. The day of the trustees meeting I was in the office early, sipping Dunkin' Donuts jet fuel, but before the day was over I knew I'd be moving into a potato vodka martini on the rocks with four olives.

That's my beverage of choice at cocktail hour. When I'm out at dinner the olives come in handy in case I run into a prissy chef whose menus feature rare roasted parrot on a bed of cranberry sauce and minced rodent lettuce wrap.

I confess that I concentrated so much on football, I was late jumping on the basketball train. I didn't realize what had been going on in college hoops. But one day I noticed it was apparently legal for players to take five steps and carry the ball before they fed it to the rim. I also discovered that women like hoops. They can see the athletes. The players aren't covered up in helmets, face masks, and armor. And the game's not complicated. Fill up the other team's bucket more than it fills up yours.

I especially liked the fact that hoops was cheaper than football. You only provide scholarships for thirteen kids instead of eighty-five. To build a winner, the two athletes you most need are a shooting guard who comes with a 3 that don't get broke, and a seven-foot goon who can rebound without falling down—even if he's a Chinaman who likes to eat fish heads.

I had to retire our longtime coach, "Kindly Doc" Shaffer, for going to sleep during games, for having only two winning seasons in fifteen years, and for neglecting to tell his players to attend class.

I replaced him with Flip Dixon. I lured Flip away from Arkansas Tech. Tops in his resume was that he'd never been caught cheating. He wore checkered sports coats and striped ties like a movie gangster in the thirties. I told him I'd never understood why hoops coaches dress in coats and ties at games. They should wear sweaters like Coach Bob Knight when he was leading Indiana to three national championships.

Flip Dixon said, "Let me win a national championship and I'll dress like Coach Knight."

Flip has taken the Big U. to the regionals twice, but he complains about bad luck. That's what he calls being unable to keep a top player on the campus longer than one or two seasons. The kid will say he didn't sign up to play "class," he signed up to play hoops—and leaves for the NBA.

I'm proud to say I've been a good friend to women's sports. I didn't complain about Title IX after I became AD in 2003. I've added six new NCAA sports for women, and this included beach volleyball after I watched it on TV in the 2008 Olympics. And I couldn't resist teasing the board. I said I was gonna design the uniforms myself, and at the moment I was leaning toward the *Sports Illustrated* swimsuit issue look.

I have to say the best thing that happened during my reign as far as the trustees were concerned was the football team's performance two years ago in the Aunt Jemima Buttermilk Pancake Mix Sugar Bowl.

We narrowly missed out on the four-team playoff for the national championship. We only lost one game that season, but the selection committee, ever vigilant of TV ratings, chose Michigan, Alabama, Oklahoma, and Notre Dame over us, the Irish despite two losses.

A TV executive explained the choices: "Those teams bring more romance to the dance," he said seriously.

Being left out was a cruel disappointment for our kids and fans, but it wasn't a complete loss for my appetite. Not when I stopped to think about oysters on the half shell at Felix's, the *trout meunière* topped with lump crab at Galatoire's, and Louisiana red beans and rice inside any doorway with a neon sign. New Orleans is the only foreign country I enjoy visiting where nobody speaks English.

Coach Tag had our team ready. We outscored the Auburn Tigers 49 to 42 in a thriller in the Superdome. On top of the win, a member of the bowl committee told me our fans had set a sustenance record in the French Quarter that week.

After the game there was a scene in the Quarter that none of us on hand would soon forget. It was the sight of our esteemed chancellor, Dr. Warren Carpenter, on a corner of Bourbon Street after having been substantially overserved while celebrating our victory. There he was, struggling to hold on to a lamp post with one hand while trying to pull up his pants with the other.

Ah, hell, I can tell you stories all day long.

TWO

ONE STORY I dine out on is how I acquired my name of Pete Wallace. I mean my first name. My last name was always Wallace. I basically became Pete because my daddy couldn't pronounce "Perseus."

My mama Blanche named me after her daddy, Perseus, who was about half Greek. It happened that she named me while my own daddy, Darnell, was busy in his auto repair shop changing the suspension springs on a '55 Chevy Bel Air and didn't make it to the hospital in time to argue about it.

My dad never learned how to say Perseus. He'd hit all round it—"Pur-see-liss" was as close as he came—which is why he started calling me Pete.

The on-and-off argument about my name lasted through grade school, and I made it easy on them by answering to both.

I'd be playing outside while my mama was watering the yard with a garden hose and she would holler, "Perseus, if that baseball breaks a window in this house, your butt's gonna be redder than a Christmas sweater!"

At dinner Darnell would say, "Pete, if you're not gonna get after that other pork chop, you want to donate it to your daddy's pork chop fund?"

One day I heard my dad say to my mom, "If you was dead-set on giving him a Greek name, why couldn't you go with something short enough for people to say, like, you know, Zeus or Nero?"

Blanche said, "Darnell, sometimes I think you *try* to be dumb."

Darnell said, "I'll tell you who's dumb. Them Greeks. They walked around in bedsheets with grapes on their head and slept in a pile of ruins. That's all I know about it."

Blanche said, "Darnell. Nero wasn't a damn Greek. *Nero* was a Roman—and you can take that to the bank today this minute . . . stop laughing, Perseus."

I wanted to look more like a Pete than a Perseus growing up, and I think I do today. I was six feet tall by the time I reached high school, but I was sturdy. And I've managed to stay fit through the years as best I can without turning into a psycho gym-rat lunatic.

◼ ◼ ◼

IF A MAN writes a book, which I might someday, people usually want to know something about the author. Like, does he come from somewhere, is he a real person, and can they be sure pussy hasn't ruined his brain.

I'm from deep West Texas. Out there where the owls hump the chickens. Our town was Sandy Creek. The creek strongly resembled its name.

We weren't so rural that we didn't have a high school football team, and I was part of it. I didn't make all-county or anything, but folks said I "tried hard."

We were the Sandy Creek Prairie Dogs, but one day in workout I got picked up and thrown away by a big old tackle named Travis Mackery. Shaking it off, I said, "Dang, they ought to call us the Fightin' Front-End Loaders."

That was how Travis Mackery got his nickname of "Front End." But that wasn't the only thing that made Travis famous in town. Late one night he broke into the stadium and stole a football game jersey and a pair of Coach Hank Woodall's sneakers. Then he stupidly wore the jersey and the sneakers to school. When the coach saw Travis in a hall wearing the football jersey and his personal sneakers, he momentarily resigned from the human race to become something akin to a werewolf.

Coach Woodall marched Travis out onto the front lawn of the school and made him strip down to his jock while we watched. He made Travis walk two blocks over to the Dairy Queen and bring him back a cheeseburger and a strawberry milkshake. Then he ran Travis's coveralls up the flagpole where they flew beneath the Stars and Stripes and the Lone Star for a brief spell.

The only other time I saw Coach Woodall that angry was when his wife Jackie caught him kissing Paula Bishop behind a counter in Francine's Fashions on Broad Street. Paula worked there selling dresses. While folks watched, Jackie kicked the coach out into the street and kept kicking him until her shoe came off.

The coach called a squad meeting the next day to share a "life lesson" with us. We crowded into his office, which smelled like aftershave, and he said, "Boys, women is apt to be a problem as you go through life. I want you to know I didn't nail Paula Bishop, she nailed *me*. And all I got to say about that is, what else is there to do for fun in this piss-poor town?"

I was a good-enough halfback that I earned a scholarship to the Texas College of Fine Arts & Ranching. Texas FA&R. The campus was in Grub, Texas, which wasn't far from Sandy Creek, to pin it down for you.

People think football players only study sports in college, but I studied American history, and learned about the heroes who had something to do with it—Davy Crockett, Robert E. Lee,

Teddy Roosevelt, General Patton, and others. Kids don't learn this now. They learn "social history." World War II, the most incredible event in the history of mankind, is lucky to get one chapter in today's textbooks. Meanwhile three chapters are devoted to the "valiant" college students who shut down campuses to protest the Vietnam War.

You wouldn't have wanted to discuss this with my daddy. He was eighteen years old when he joined the army in '43. He couldn't wait to go kill Nazis and Japs. By the fall of '44 he was a private in an infantry battalion of the 1st Infantry Division. They fought through France, Belgium, and Germany.

Daddy remembered shooting at windows in buildings and trees in a forest, and getting shot at in return. He hoped he hit some "gray suits." He was lucky to come home in one piece with a Combat Infantry Badge, a Silver Star, Bronze Star, two Purple Hearts, and pride in what he'd done.

Darnell recalled the sixties. I was only six going on fifteen, having been born in 1961, and he never forgot how the students protested on television. TV loves protests and my dad said TV had encouraged college students to protest instead of going to whip the commies. It was TV that persuaded college kids that it was more patriotic to fight for America by staying home, smoking dope, and fucking hippies.

■ ■ ■

I LEARNED the "Gunga Din" poem in college. I only learned "*Où est Passé Roger?*" in French class but got a passing grade because I played football. Same with business class. "Lessee" and "lessor" was about it. And I cheated through math, as did everybody else I knew. Nobody knows fractions. Bankers make up that one and three-eighths bullshit.

Sandy Creek and Grub are both gone now. My high school is gone, Texas FA&R and the football stadium are gone. So is everything else—homes, streets, the park, the country club. The oil and natural gas people invaded and converted the whole area into a mess of derricks, drilling rigs, storage tanks, and trucks.

I was off chasing after my own career when it took place, and it was sad to come home on a visit in the nineties and find that everything I'd known didn't exist anymore, other than a mesquite tree here and there.

Most people don't know how you find natural gas. I have an idea. They stick a long steel pipe down in the ground and let it set off a nuclear bomb. This cracks open a gigantic layer of rock and lets out the gas that's been trapped down there since a dinosaur farted. When the gas rises up to ground level, workers run around snatching buckets and pails of it to take to the storage tanks, where it stays until Exxon turns it into energy.

My folks didn't mind the natural gas boom. The house where I grew up and my daddy's auto repair shop happened to be sitting on top of it. Blanche got a Lexus out of the deal and Darnell got a Range Rover and the royalties bought them a brick house in Abilene, which Blanche called "closer to civilization."

They enjoyed a good life there before they died, and I choose to think that Blanche passed on with a smile, knowing that she hadn't spent the last years of her life having to drive fifty miles to a Walmart, Target, or Best Buy.

THREE

IN MY well-traveled youth I probably coached on more college campuses than your average Texan goes to gun shows in a year.

For better or worse, I was determined to make a living in sports. It was the only thing I cared about. Let grownups sell insurance.

I spent my twenties as an assistant football coach at some curious places, but I was happy to be employed. At first I coached every position and picked up equipment and bagged the trash, but I studied my craft, got along with people, and eventually was hired as the offensive coordinator at Southern Dunes College in Three Farms, Nebraska, which had some dunes but no farmhouses I ever saw.

Compared to where I'd worked, which was from remote Arkansas to hidden Montana and back again, Southern Dunes seemed like the Ivy League to me. However, it wouldn't be much of an exaggeration to say that we practiced among bales of hay and played our home games on a field of sawdust.

Southern Dunes was a job I was happy to have, but it didn't pay enough for me to afford a house. I lived in a Road Warrior motor home that towed my Ford Granada. My kitchen was a hot plate, the bathroom was the closet, and the windows looked out on vending machines in a roadside park. I dined on White Castle to Arby's cuisine, but I'd treat myself to a big breakfast on Sundays at a Cracker Barrel or Waffle House—if my car had enough gas in it.

I wasn't without lady friends in my travels. I discovered that if you're single and don't have any visible sores, the lookers will throw a net over you. I met most of my ladies when I played recreational tennis in my spare time to keep in shape. You may remember when tennis was a craze in America. It's my theory that the tennis craze wore off when American men stopped winning "Wimpleton," as some of our football coaches refer to it today.

Pam, Lou, and Cheryl. Man, there were three first-round selections.

I thought I was about half in love with Pam in Arkadelphia, Arkansas, until I grew tired of watching her burst into tears out of nowhere for reasons she never explained and would get mad because I couldn't figure it out.

I thought I was about one-third in love with Lou in Bozeman, Montana, until she started making me look at furniture in a store window.

And I thought I was two-thirds in love with Cheryl in Natchitoches, Louisiana, until she started heaving these long sighs when we'd be alone and I'd be reading the paper. I'd ask what was wrong and she'd get mad like Pam did.

I tried to end those romances on a friendly basis, although Pam said she felt like an Alka-Seltzer tablet that had been dropped in a glass of faucet water.

◾ ◾ ◾

I'D TURNED thirty when I was offered the head football coach's job at Flat Beach State in Flat Beach, North Carolina. My second season we won the Shoreline Conference, but Hurricane Royce blew away the trophy and one side of my pre-fab office with it.

But I'll always have a soft spot for Flat Beach. It is where I met Glenda Boyd, my wife of twenty-two years.

The first time I saw Glenda I was driving past the practice range at Windy Cove Country Club. She was hitting golf balls and looking serious about it, like it was more of a job than a sport.

Glenda was curvy in the right places, a brunette with her hair worn in a bob, and overall pretty enough that I couldn't resist making a move on her. I walked over, introduced myself, and . . .

"Mark your lip," she said curtly. "I'm working on my draw."

Golf banter.

I liked her spunk.

She was born in Flat Beach, had played on the women's golf team for four years, and graduated with a degree in physical therapy. She was the club champion at Windy Cove and the city champion of Flat Beach. We began going out and, if anything, my interest increased after I met her parents.

Her mama Evelyn, an attractive lady, and her dad Glen Tom, a friendly guy, owned and ran a drugstore on a corner near the campus. He was the pharmacist, she the bookkeeper. They'd inherited the drugstore from Evelyn's parents and kept it thriving. Glenda worked there three or four days a week to support her golf habit.

I was amused that Glenda's daddy didn't understand what I did for a living. He said, "What do you mean you *coach*?"

I tried to describe it in more detail, or thought I did.

Glen Tom said, "So you just stand around and tell people where to line up or sit down in a circle or run off somewhere and come back?"

"That's about it," I said with a smile.

He said, "Huh. I don't like team sports, Pete. Never watch 'em. Fishing and hunting are my games, and I don't need somebody to coach me how to do it, no offense to you."

I worked my way around to proposing to Glenda. She said she'd always wanted to be in love, or something similar, but I would have to accept her terms if she consented to marry me. Her terms were, she didn't want to have children, ever—she'd rather have dogs—and she insisted on us living near a golf course. So what about it?

We were married in a non-denominational church in Flat Beach, the kind that had a jazz band. The preacher played the clarinet in the band and expected everybody in the congregation to drop $20 in the hat every Sunday or burn in hell forever.

Glenda insisted we honeymoon in Mexico City. She'd seen pictures of Club de Golf, a course she wanted to play because history said Ben Hogan and Arnold Palmer had made it famous. And she wanted to see the Aztec ruins in and around the city. See if they were as old as they pretended to be.

I tried to tell her that only three things can happen to you if you visit Mexico. You can get robbed, you can get kidnapped, and you can get *tourista*.

I got hit with *tourista* the minute I stepped off the plane. And Glenda never played a round of golf. A scorpion the size of my brown loafer stung her on the toe the first night we were in our hotel room.

■ ■ ■

DEALING with football players on the level of Flat Beach State was a test of my patience. Some were so dumb they'd call timeout in a game to ask me what the play was. They encouraged me to think I might be better suited for the administrative side of things.

I took a shot at applying for the assistant athletic director's job at Morris Union College in Forest Grove, Tennessee. The athletic director was Zeke Hollis, who doubled as the town mayor and was somebody I rarely saw, leaving me to do his job for him. He'd hired me after I told him I had my own car.

Everybody in Forest Grove lived in a log cabin, and so did we, but ours was the smallest. One bedroom, living room, kitchen, bath. Glenda was sure that some of the logs weren't fitted properly. She felt drafts.

My wife found out ahead of time that the town had a golf course or I might not have taken the job. The clubhouse was a log cabin at Raccoon Mountain Golf Club. The dining room specialized in country ham, red-eye gravy, and biscuits. But you could order eggs if you didn't mind waiting for Larry the cook to get off the phone. Lunch was limited to soft drinks, a bowl of chili, hotdogs, hamburgers, a sack of Fritos, and fried pies. I found nothing wrong with the menu, but Glenda brought her own tuna fish sandwiches.

A group of men hung out every day at the club, but none of them cared to play nine or eighteen holes with Glenda. They weren't even polite about it.

One of the men bluntly said to my wife, "Wimmin people have no place on a golf course—except for the beer bitch in the beverage cart."

Wimmin people.

I thought that was funnier than Glenda did.

Wimmin People and the Beer Bitch.

Perfect movie title to attract the millennials.

Glenda was grateful that I didn't stay at Morris Union long enough to find out who Morris was.

After a year and a half, I received an offer to become the athletic director at Great Sioux State in Bison River, South Dakota. I was recommended by the president of Flat Beach State. He and the president of Great Sioux State were friends from going on church junkets with their wives to look at leaves changing.

I said to Glenda I wasn't going to miss people telling me that if it hadn't been for Tennessee, there wouldn't have been a Texas. She said the only thing she'd miss about Tennessee was not leaving sooner.

She said, "This state will keep you fit. I'll swear to that. You have to walk uphill to go anywhere, and walk uphill coming back from going anywhere."

Great Sioux State was a move upward and my first chance to be the real boss. I jumped at the offer without asking if I had to wear war paint and kill my own food.

We rented a two-bedroom stucco house nearer to the Lakota Country Club than it was to the campus. The course was surprisingly lush. Green fairways with trees and shrubs everywhere. It was named for the Oglala Lakota tribe that was led by Red Cloud in its days of glory. Red Cloud was the school's mascot. He was also a legend. A Plains Indian who'd done his share of damage to various United States cavalry regiments—some of it on the very spot where the golf course was built.

Glenda was thrilled to find a golf course of such "out-of-place elegance" in a part of the country where she'd expected to find the greens made out of sand and the rough full of cactus, rocks, and Gila monsters.

FOUR

I PUMPED life into the football program at Great Sioux State from the start. I coached the team the first year while simultaneously looking after the AD job. The school had already fired Coach Tubby Stockbridge for two reasons: not winning enough games and outweighing most of his linemen.

What I did first was borrow a bunch of athletes from the school's championship rodeo team and explain to them that wrestling a steer, tying down a calf, or staying on a saddle bronc for eight seconds wasn't much different from sneak-holding on offense. They took to it real quick.

I hired Bucko Martin as the head coach the second year. He'd been a loyal assistant at Flat Beach State, and he kept the engine running. Bucko growled louder than me. But I discovered that if you work at a school where the mascot is Red Cloud, you can count on being assaulted by a group of protesters.

The protesters will get around to attacking you after they've worn themselves out trying to change the name of the Washington Redskins to the Washington Transsexual Reassignment Survivors.

As far as that goes, I want it on record here and now that I am not in the least offended if the name of the New York Giants is hurtful to midgets. We're talking about *sports teams*, for Christ's sake.

The small group of protesters who showed up pretended to be overly distressed that we were the Red Clouds. They said they were concerned Native Americans, which was interesting since the six of them were white as me. They demanded that we change the Red Clouds to a mascot they could live with, for instance, the Shetland Ponies.

I've been sick of political correctness since I first noticed it. Which was when two great universities, Stanford and Dartmouth, caved in to the busybodies and changed their mascots from gallant Indian braves to Crayolas, or whatever they call themselves now.

When one of the agitators called me insensitive, I kept my composure. I said, "You want to be a real Indian, buy a headdress. I'm a 'Native American.' That's what you are if you're born in the USA like I was, like my parents were, and like my great-grandparents were, and all my relatives as far back as you want to go till you hit Scotland and Ireland. But I've never burned a village, attacked a wagon train, or scalped a paleface, even when I was drinking."

The agitator was a scruffy guy in his thirties who wore his ball cap sideways, a clear indication that he was an intellectual.

I said, "By the way. I still haven't forgiven your Comanches for kidnapping Natalie Wood and holding her hostage until every Indian was given his own casino."

It was the highlight of my stay in South Dakota.

Truth is, I never thought I'd wind up living in the Midwest. But sixteen years ago Western Ohio University grew tired of dominating the Mid-Continent Conference and aimed to upgrade its athletic program and strive to enter a major conference. I was plucked out of South Dakota to help lead the way.

Roy Clapper was head of the search committee and he liked the job I'd done at Great Sioux State for three years. He'd looked into my record and saw that I'd taken a job at a place where you couldn't win, but did.

I was happy to find Shackayooka one of the prettiest college towns in America. It took its name from the Indian tribe that spun itself off from the Chippewa. This was after the U.S. 3rd Cavalry whipped up on the Chippewa in the Battle of Spotted Dog Creek. There are historic markers everywhere in town to tell you about it.

I served under lovable Amos Alonzo Howell for a year and a half. Amos arrived at the Big U. around the same time that frozen dinners arrived in America. I felt I would replace him sooner than later. The day I got there Amos was hobbling around on a cane with dabs of mac and cheese on his necktie.

My first year was devoted to helping Amos find his eyeglasses, answering to him calling me "Preston," and listening to him complain about his wife Essie reading the newspaper out loud.

I succeeded Amos after he passed away from heart failure. He took his leave in the middle of the night. Essie said the old goat woke up unexpectedly, raised himself up in bed, hollered out "Interference," and slumped back down, "deader than a stepped-on bug."

Essie scattered his ashes on the stadium turf and fulfilled Amos's wish to have words on his tombstone that would last forever. She wrote them herself. The tombstone reads:

Here lies Amos Alonzo Howell. He gave his heart,
Remington typewriter, and football luncheons to Western
Ohio University. Go Cheetahs.

So there we were in the Midwest on our second poodle, who was named Marissa, like the first one, because that's what Glenda wished her parents had named her, and our first English springer spaniel, who was named Clive because it sounded English. Clive was more expensive than her new set of golf clubs.

■ ■ ■

MIDWESTERNERS are good folks, I was pleased to discover. They may not be as fast as Texans to poke fun at themselves, but they have a sense of humor you don't need to dig around to find. They take pride in their football, hardware stores, drugstores, diners, meat markets, filling stations, and roasting ears.

I'll take Midwesterners over most of the people I know from—well, New England, just to pull a place out of a tri-cornered hat.

I like Boston as a city even though Locke-Ober's restaurant is gone. Fenway Park is still holding on. So is the old concrete Harvard Stadium, the first collegiate football stadium built in the United States in 1903. I have good friends in and from Boston.

But I don't know about the rest of New England. Your Vermonts and New Hampshires and your Cape Cods. Too many of them want to stop and hug a tree when they're going somewhere. And the rest of them don't seem completely comfortable unless they're sitting in furniture that still creaks from all the Benjamin Franklins who sat in them.

You can't go up against their maple syrup, though.

FIVE

I'VE HAD a secret weapon in this job. The secret weapon's name is Rita Jo Foster. Any success I've had as the AD couldn't have happened without the help and support of Rita Jo. Fresh out of the Big U. with a degree in communications, she started as my secretary and rapidly worked her way up to my deputy assistant because she's super-smart, trustworthy, creative—and a knockout.

Rita Jo is a blue-eyed blonde who can hold her own with those smokin' hot babes on *Fox News*. She's a stunner who tends to wear her skirts too many inches above the knee for the approval of church ladies. But she can turn up in a pair of jeans you'd swear were painted on. Those jeans show off a set of wheels that would stand out in any chorus line. She goes about five ten in heels.

It's also true that I've found those attributes more than mildly distracting. But Rita Jo is only a friend and confidante. My wife and Rita Jo get along in public, but at home Glenda likes to refer to her as my "little girlfriend." And she wonders when Rita Jo is going to discover the pantsuit.

Rita Jo comes from an upper-middle-class family in Cincinnati. Her folks are college grads and fun to be with when they visit. Her father, Ryan, had been an editor of various sections of the *Cincinnati Enquirer* until he retired. Her mother, Naomi, was an excellent feature writer on the same paper.

She has a nifty relationship with her parents and her older sister, Rachel, a prominent obstetrician in Cincinnati. Mom, dad, sister, and Rita Jo stay close by phone and other means of electricity, and Rita Jo goes to see them every chance she gets. It's an enviable family by any measure.

Amazingly, my two young stud assistants, Mike Hodges and Rick Adams, have never made a move on Rita Jo. I gathered she was too old for them. Rita Jo is into her middle thirties now, although she looks and plays much younger. Mike and Rick were more inclined to take aim at the scantily clad Cheetah Girls, or make periodic runs on the Chi Omega house.

It bewildered me that Rita Jo had never married. When she was in her twenties I kept thinking a dish like her would be buckled down in a private jet any minute and hauled off to a villa in France. She occasionally enjoyed what she called a "Citation Weekend," but said she'd yet to meet a gentleman attractive and interesting enough to make her want to marry.

She confessed that marital opportunities with rich guys had presented themselves, but she wasn't interested in becoming a "California wife." A California wife, she said, was a woman with nothing to do but shop, drink, sunbathe, and say "motherfucker" a lot.

Rita Jo's dates may have been good dancers but they were worthless jerks in my opinion. She'd bring them around for me to size up. The Eastwood types had names like Skeet, Slugger, and Carl. The Wall Street wet-heads came with names like Shep, Dace, and Rog. I asked her one day to look around and see if she couldn't find a James or a Robert somewhere in the crowd.

Some of the aces she brought around were generous enough to invite me to invest in their get-rich-quick schemes.

I'm not likely to forget Skeet Tims. He was developing a donut and wonton take-out and intended to lease a space in a shopping mall that hadn't been built yet on a stretch of new highway under construction south of town.

Skeet said, "It's a can't-miss deal. Old people like donuts, young people like wonton. We'll split the investment right down the middle. My brains and your money."

Slugger Holland was another one. He showed up wearing a black blazer with gold buttons, unfolded a map, and said he was going to make us rich after I paid his expenses to go down to Paraguay and get us in on "this gold rush deal."

■ ■ ■

WHEN Rita Jo became my deputy assistant, I needed a new secretary. I've had three in ten years. The first two didn't want to be bothered if they were reading Danielle Steel novels. The winner, Francine Noble, is a nice lady in her sixties. She answers my angry letters, she never complains, and protects my doorway from everybody but Rita Jo. Francine doesn't gossip, doesn't want to chat, doesn't want to be my friend. The only thing she's ever revealed to me about her private life is that her husband Wayne didn't tell her he liked liver and onions until after they were married.

■ ■ ■

RITA JO and I discussed what her future might hold after I retire. She knows, as I do, that the guy who replaces me will want to bring in his own people. He will say, "I want to make my own mistakes," having read it in a book on how to succeed in business.

She insists I don't have to worry about her. TV stations in Cincinnati and Columbus had tried to hire her to sit at a desk and read the sports news. She might consider that. But her first choice was to stay connected with the university in some executive position, and she had let this be known to Roy Clapper. Recently she told me that ideally she'd like to try again to start up a sports marketing department at the Big U., and run it herself.

She said, "I'm sure I don't have to remind you that most sports marketing people are throw-aways."

"Tell me about it," I grinned.

Three years ago Roy Clapper suggested we "modernize." He ordered me to hire a marketing firm headquartered in Washington, D.C. The firm sent us three young women and a young man. I managed to arrange offices for them in the hoops dome.

They started off by ordering new furniture and wall covering for their offices, and delighting in three-hour lunches. Then they began to hold four-hour meetings with design consultants they'd bring in from New York.

When I inquired what they were working on one day, the guy said, "You may not have noticed that it's a new world out there, old-timer. We don't send out flyers in the mail anymore. There's something called the Internet."

I said, "I'll keep that to myself. Try not to spread it around. It could throw us all out of rhythm around here."

I had misgivings about the four of them from the start, largely because the young women, Allison, Bipsy, and Jazzy, had attended a girls' school in Virginia, where they majored in Eggs Benedict. The young guy, Timmy, had played lacrosse or something at some Eastern college that came up short on ivy. Their constant smug expressions struck me as out of place since none of their daddies were U.S. ambassadors to countries I'd almost heard of.

After six months of creative meetings they presented me with six suggestions they were extremely proud of. In order of their absurdity, they were: Replace "The Star-Spangled Banner" before the kickoff with "We Are the World." Show our support for same-sex marriage with messages on the Jumbotron. Print our football tickets pink with cartoon drawings of female football players on them. Give the band a hip-hop arrangement of our fight song. For three of the six home games each season, have a Muslim leader give the pre-game invocation in Arabic. Invite men and transgenders to become part of the Cheetah Girls and change the name of the dance team to the "Cheetah Diversifieds."

I said, "Those ideas sound interesting. I'll get back to you after I'm waterboarded."

The last straw was their proposal of a sign to appear on billboards around the town and countryside. It would become our slogan. The sign would say: "Up the Big. U!"

I called the four of them in and calmly tried to explain how the slogan could possibly—just possibly—be taken the wrong way.

Then I fired the nitwits.

SIX

IF THERE'S a downside to having a winning football program, it's the risk of your head coach becoming a prima donna—not that he'd start dressing like he was in an opera. Mainly he'd begin to demand things he hadn't thought of before.

First off came the coach's announcement that he wanted free automobiles for his coaching staff and himself. There should be boosters in town who'd want to become "part of the team" by providing the new cars on an annual basis.

Talk Big's staff had multiplied to outnumber the population of some of the towns I'd lived in. It consisted of Chick Overstock, the offensive coordinator; Red Stages, defensive coordinator; Burt Crouch, offensive line coach; Marv Booker, defensive line coach; Gus Murray, running backs coach; Hog Elliott, linebackers coach; Bobby Skinner, safeties coach; Hub Burkett, cornerbacks coach; Buster Dibbs, wide receivers coach; Floyd Tarlton, tight ends coach; Jake Sawyer, special teams coach; Moose Cook, strength and conditioning coach; Mac Dunn, athletic trainer; Ben Tolbert, director of football operations; Brice Lewis, video coordinator; and Talk Big's secretary, Ruthie Summers, a pleasant but naïve woman in her sixties. Ruthie held another title: "Director of Humanitarian Affairs." Sounded better than Bag Lady.

If you don't know what a Bag Lady is in collegiate athletics, she's the person who dips into a slush fund and doles out cash to football and basketball players "in need." It's never surprising how many needy athletes there are.

Most of Coach Tag's demands fell on Rita Jo to handle. But she never complained.

Surprisingly, she took care of the automobile request without much trouble. That I knew of. She somehow wormed eight Buick Veranos out of Lance Murphy, a car dealer, and she sweet-talked Shifty Conroy, another dealer, out of eight Cadillac Escalades. The staff played Ping-Pong to see who got which. Talk Big took one of each.

She also dealt with the wishes of Connie Taggert, the coach's wife, who had never gotten over the fact that she was once a Miss Fiberglass Drywall Tape 400 on the NASCAR circuit in Corndale, Iowa. Connie wanted a new master bathroom and adjoining spa for their home. It had to be done twice to please her.

Connie might have been a beauty queen in her younger days, but that was before her numerous do-overs gave her slits for eyes and lips like Mick Jagger. It pains me to say it, but today she comes closer to looking like one of the *Real Housewives of Antarctica*.

In an effort to hold down the cost, Rita Jo agreed to have dinner with the contractor, Floyd Spooner. He confessed to being recently divorced and lonely. After dinner, Floyd suggested he rent a room at the River View Motel where he would show her his Desert Storm wounds from his days in combat, her being a patriot. Rita Jo declined, saying she was fighting a skin rash. Prior research had told her that Floyd was married with two young children.

Rita Jo took charge when Talk Big wanted to find a craftsman to design and build him an ebony-inlaid conference room table with a cheetah engraved in gilt in the middle of the table. It would be good for his staff's morale when they sat around in meetings.

Rita Jo found a craftsman in Wisconsin to do it for a price that would have bought us two good linebackers. I don't know that the carving in the table looks as much like a cheetah as it does a block of cheese on four legs, but the coach likes it.

Next it became Rita Jo's chore to oversee the remodeling of the coach's office. Coach Tag insisted on enlarging the two small windows in the office to become one giant window that provided a sweeping view of the football field. He also demanded a recreational alcove for a treadmill and stationary bike, and a wall-sized TV screen on which to study game videos.

Not to overlook a prominent spot for a large stuffed cheetah, the one he shot on a hunting safari in Namibia. The coach had not tracked the animal across the bush in a sporting fashion. Instead he set up a blind near a watering hole and waited hours with his buddies, telling jokes and sipping whiskey, until the cheetah showed up thirsty, at which point everybody blasted away. But Coach Tag took credit for the kill.

■ ■ ■

WE ENDURED an unfortunate period involving our football uniforms until Rita Jo and I collaborated to put an end to it.

NewJock, Inc. had been designing our uniforms, and for marketing reasons of their own, the company thought it was doing us a favor by starting to dress our team somewhat peculiarly. Talk Big put up with it because the company provided free trips to Vegas every year for himself and six of his buddies.

I was stunned the day the coach came in my office and said the company intended to spice up our uniforms even more so with a third color on the jerseys.

"What color might that be?" I asked.

"Baby blue," he said.

"Baby blue?" I said with a look.

"They call it an accent," he said.

"You're saying *baby blue*," I said. "Baby blue to go with our traditional orange and tan?"

He said, "That's their idea. Baby blue stripes on the shoulders and sleeves."

I said, "Well, Coach, I haven't been to every zoo in America, but I've been to my share, and I don't think I've ever seen a limpwrist cheetah."

The remark made no impression on him.

NewJock, Inc. kept on toying with our uniforms until they did away with our school colors altogether. Our jerseys began to look like we were flying the flags of Mozambique and Slovakia. Our pants resembled three flavors of Baskin-Robbins, and they put us in helmets that reminded me, personally, of a pepperoni pizza.

I broke army barracks–cussing records and Rita Jo stood by me when we told the coach we couldn't tolerate this any longer. He should read the angry letters and emails and Twitter comments my office was receiving.

The nicest email was this one:

If Coach Brain Dead is going to dress our football players
like clowns, they damn well better keep winning.

We insisted that we dump NewJock and he could say goodbye to Vegas. Rita Jo would find another equipment company that would send the coach and his buddies on free trips to Macao or the Bahamas or the WinStar casino and resort in Thackerville, Oklahoma, wherever that was.

Rita Jo switched us over to Uni-Up and that's how we returned to looking familiar again. As in orange jerseys with white numerals, tan helmets, and tan pants at home, and white jerseys with orange numerals, orange pants, and tan helmets on the road.

The head of Uni-Up, a man named Claude Dugger, came to town in person to sign the contract with us. I let Rita Jo iron out the details with him. It included giving the company a little wiggle room with stripes and numerals on designing our uniforms as long as the company's designer stuck with our basic orange and tan colors. Their meeting went smoothly. I asked Rita Jo how she managed to close the deal so quickly.

She said, "Oh, I just met him in his suite at the Grand Palace downtown in my fishnet stockings, spike heels, garter belt, and sailor hat. The rest was easy."

She was obviously joking. But sometimes I wondered.

SEVEN

WHILE I was waiting to hear from the trustees that day, I had expected a mid-morning call from Glenda asking if we were rich yet. But no call came. Golf was holding her hostage again, I figured.

My wife had a habit of calling when I was in the middle of something. Like the day I was in a budget negotiation with Roy Clapper. She called to tell me she knew I was never interested in her activities, but I could reach her on her cell today if I needed her—she was teeing off in the tournament in ten minutes.

"What tournament?" I asked.

She said, "'What tournament?' Jesus. We haven't talked about it, have we? The Bent Oak Women's Team Championship. We intend to win it."

I asked who "we" were.

She said, "I've told you. Cassandra Stewart, Lucinda Knox, and Belinda Baker."

I said, "Glenda, Cassandra, Lucinda, and Belinda. That lineup would strike fear in anybody."

Five hours later she called to let me in on the exciting news that her foursome had indeed won the event. She and Cassandra, Lucinda, and Belinda had dethroned "the Bent Oak Bitches," as she had named the perennial champions, Vivien, Donna, Lilah, and Mildred.

"High fives all around," I said.

She started off telling me how she gave her team a big boost with a great second shot at the first hole, and how she followed that up with a terrific putt for a birdie at the second hole.

I sensed that I was about to hear details of her entire round, so I interrupted her to say, "Glenda, if you're gonna take me the whole eighteen, I'm gonna have to have caddie fees."

Silence for a moment. Then she said: "Is your little girlfriend there with you today?"

I said, "No, my *deputy* . . . and the rest of my staff are off to do other things while I deal with Roy."

Glenda said, "Well, if I need Rita for anything later on, where should I look? Will she be shopping in the sexy lingerie department at Nordstrom or meeting with her Bible study group?"

I don't have a good record of topping my wife in a wise-ass contest, but she hung up before I could try.

EIGHT

ACTUALLY, the first call I received was from Eddie Ralph Stoddard, lawyer to rich people only, one of my moles on the board. No AD is worth his weight in three-piece suits unless he has two moles on the board. Roy Clapper, my other mole, was busy presiding.

Eddie Ralph called to say they hadn't taken up my retirement yet. They were stalled in a debate on whether to grant life tenure to three professors who'd been organizing uppity foreign students to raise hell on their behalf. Eddie Ralph was sure I could guess who the professors were. I could.

One was sure to be Dr. Irene Randolph Richardson, an English professor who taught a course called The Non-White Novel, and a second course labeled Hemingway and the Overrated Caucasians.

Another one had to be Dr. Foroud Azad, our very own Iranian. He taught a popular course called Disguises, Bombs, Weapons and the Fun of Terrorism.

The third one could only be Dr. Phouc Huu, our North Vietnamese scholar. His specialty was a course in American imperialism, and he had authored a best-selling memoir with a catchy title: *Hey, Yank—Your Napalm Cooked My Breakfast.*

I told Eddie Ralph I recommended torture over tenure. Severe torture. Like lock them in a room and make them listen to rap till they beg for mercy.

NINE

IF YOU were to ask most people in this town when I started to look smarter than a man who'd got himself born to rich parents, they'll tell you it was when I finally fired Weldon "Warthog" Price as our football coach and replaced him with Coach Tag.

Dumping Warthog became more of an ordeal than I'd anticipated.

He coached the Cheetahs for 16 years, but he'd only turned out three winning teams, and the best of those was a 7-5 season helped along by foul-weather Saturdays and favored opponents showing up with injuries to their top players.

Talk Big had been Warthog's offensive coordinator for the last five of his seasons. Not that he was allowed to do any offensive coordinating. Warthog believed wholeheartedly in defense and relied on the cliché, "Offense wins games, defense wins championships." This was strange since Warthog had never won a championship, even as a high school coach in Springfield, Illinois.

Talk Big begged Warthog to let him re-design the offense.

"We have to go vertical," he'd say. "Passing and speed, that's the future."

Warthog would snarl his standard response: "Passing ain't football. Football is a man's game played down in the trenches, stink on stink."

Warthog refused to resign despite my offer of a generous retirement plan and a campus job with the title of Assistant to the Chancellor in Charge of Long Lunches.

But Warthog thought he was untouchable. He had a powerful friend and cheerleader in the community. The friend was Dub Spurlock, sports editor and daily columnist of the local paper, the *Clarion Tribune*. He'd been sports editor since sportswriters wore hats.

Dub Spurlock was the product of the age when the sports editor's column bore a clever name. I'd listened to scribes in bars laugh about some of the column titles in those days. The days when "The Brawn Patrol" was written by a guy in Dallas, when "Sports Off the Cob" was written by a guy in Des Moines, when "Scars and Swipes" was written by a guy in Cleveland, when "Read 'Em and Leap" was written by a guy in Miami, and when "Good Moan'in" was written by a guy in Chicago.

The head on Dub Spurlock's column was, "The Village Spigot."

Warthog and Dub became close friends from frequenting the exclusive Town Club to drink whiskey, smoke Shermans, play dominoes, generally shoot the shit, and eat the tater tot casserole. The Town Club is decorated in brass and wood and the club is older than baseball. It's where the power brokers convene to decide which people to force into bankruptcy if they don't agree to turn a beautiful public park into condos.

I became a member after I'd been at the Big U. for over a year and looked like I might have staying power. The membership was a perk for becoming the athletic director. I always used the club for lunch on Thursdays. That was beef stew day. It was on one of those beef stew days that I dined with Dub Spurlock and heard his views on modern sports writing.

As a young man, Dub had read Grantland Rice's syndicated columns and his memoir. Grantland Rice was his idol because he made every athlete out to be a hero. Grantland Rice was nothing like today's young smart-aleck sportswriters who poke fun at sports events and overpaid athletes, except those they like.

Dub said, "Sports is serious, like life. But sports can be a breath of fresh air *from* life, which is hard for most folks, what with sickness and all. Life will kick your butt if you let it. A lot of young sportswriters are pissed off at life because they hate their bosses, their wives are fat, and their kids are little snots, if not something worse. They think this gives them a license to be funny. But they're wrong. Funny is for Jack Benny and Fibber McGee. I learned this in the saddest way possible."

I didn't ask him to tell me about it because I knew he was going to.

Dub said, "One time I made fun in my column of a fellow who won a golf tournament. His swing made him turn into a pretzel, I wrote. Then I received a letter from a reader who said I had gone and taken the pleasure out of his life, and his life was a commode to start with. He had a sickly wife who stunk up the house cooking fish, and two surly kids—two surly kids who only spoke to arcade machines and computer games. He claimed his only pleasure in life was sports, but I'd gone and made fun of a golfer. I should try living his life and see sports ruined by somebody like me. I promise you that ever since that letter I have never made fun of sports. My advice to today's flippant sportswriters is, be careful with the cynical beeswax you write."

Our town lost one of its beloved characters when Dub Spurlock died in an accident on the Bent Oak golf course.

It happened when he hit a ball into the water on the right of the eighteenth green. In anger he tossed his nine iron in the water, but hastily jumped in to rescue it. That's when his foot got tangled with other clubs lying on the bottom, having suffered the same punishment for betraying their owners.

Dub couldn't pull himself loose and drowned while his playing partners were lining up their putts on the green. Nobody knew he'd drowned until his straw hat floated to the top of the pond.

Dub Spurlock was mourned by everyone in town over the age of seventy-five.

The paper offered Dub's job to Teddy Aycock, a young sportswriter on the staff of the *Clarion Tribune*. Teddy had been covering high school football. He accepted the promotion even though it meant he'd have to buy a sports coat.

To help me cut Warthog loose I summoned Roy Clapper. Roy arranged a meeting for the three of us—Roy, Warthog, and me—at his office in the Clapper Bank & Trust building. Roy's office has a large picture window behind his desk that presents a wide view of the Big U. campus, which weaves into parts of downtown. The campus and village blend together and make for a warm and pleasant atmosphere you don't find on many university campuses.

I've been on too many campuses today that have expanded so much they resemble four penitentiaries and two hospitals going to war with three high-rise parking garages. But they call it progress.

Through Roy's window you can see the red-brick football stadium that's known as Cootie Walters Field. It was built in 1930 and holds 46,000. It badly needs to be renovated and enlarged with luxury suites added, but that fundraising chore would be another AD's problem.

Cootie Walters is known as "the Father of Shackayooka." He founded the *Clarion Tribune* and made another fortune providing farmers with all the combine harvesters and tractor balers they'd ever require. A statue of Cootie greets football fans as they enter the stadium at the south end.

There's another statue at the north end, of Gibby "Four Legs" McBride, a halfback who put Western Ohio in the football headlines in the twenties. That's when Gibby ran circles around Wooster, Wabash, Case Tech, and a marvelous upset one Saturday over the Minnesota Gophers and Herb "Juice" Joesting. His statue stands at the north end of Walters Field, and the plaque reads:

> Gibby (Four Legs) McBride Built Walters Field
> As Sure As There Are Bricks and Mortar.

Other campus landmarks can be seen from Roy's office window. They stand among lush green patches of lawn and paths shaded by rows of ash, oak, and sycamore trees. You can see Babbage Hall, which the students call "Baboon Hall," and Sperry Hall, which they call "Sperm Hall," and Virginia Place, a ladies dorm, which is known to most of the male students in the parlance of college humor as "Vagina Place."

■ ■ ■

ROY STARTED off with Warthog by saying it was time for us to go in another direction. Any dummy would take that to mean he was going to be fired but Warthog showed no reaction. He leaned back in his chair and said, "I have us going in the right direction. I've taught every kid to love his parents, especially his mother and father. I know the minds of my team. I'm omnivorous."

Roy and I exchanged looks.

Warthog said, "You people don't realize how many of my defensive schemes have been copulated by other coaches in the country."

Roy and I exchanged looks again.

Roy said to Warthog that he was aware of the significant contributions the coach had made to the university, that he'd built character in the young men he'd coached, that he'd lifted the Cheetahs to a new level, but now we'd hit a wall.

Roy added, "Let's do this the easy way, coach. I know Pete has created a job for you if you wish to remain on the campus. The salary sounds reasonable to me. Or you can retire gracefully right now with a fat pension and go fishing. Live the good life. We'll let you announce your retirement in person in a press conference. What do you say?"

"I say you can stick that offer up your ass," Warthog said.

Roy Clapper stared at him. "What did you say to me?"

Warthog said, "I ain't quitting."

Roy's face turned red. "Do you know who you're talking to?"

Warthog said, "Yeah, you're the fat-ass banker in town who thinks his shit smells like a touchdown."

Roy looked at me, and said, "Did you hear that?"

"I did," I said.

Turning to Warthog, I said, "If you don't mind me saying so, Coach, you're not acting in your own best interest."

Warthog said, "I've done good things here. I have molded young men. I've had an excellent relationship with my players."

"Nobody's accusing you of having a bad relationship with your players," I said. "That's not even part of the discussion. We just think it's time for a change."

Warthog said, "Have either one of you bothered to look at the graduation rate of my football team? It's to be emanated."

Roy, stifling a grin, said, "We're aware that it's reasonably good."

Warthog said, "Only *reasonably good*? I've graduated more players than Alabama and Auburn combined!"

Roy said, "Well, who the hell hasn't?"

"I don't have to take this bullshit," Warthog said. "You people can't fire me. I have important friends in this town. Doctors. Lawyers. Normal people. I can start a riot around here. I'll sue the university."

Roy Clapper rested his arms on his desk, glared at Warthog, and said, "You'll sue the university? Go ahead. We'll tie you up in court for twenty goddamn years."

"God's on my side," Warthog said.

Roy said, "God's not a civil court judge."

Warthog slumped, and said, "So you're just gonna kick my ass out. That's what this deal is coming down to."

Roy said, "We've gone out of our way to make you two very nice offers. I'll give you one more minute to accept one of the two, or you'll leave here with nothing but your mouth and whatever you can steal from your office and the equipment room, you stupid idiot! Anything you want to add, Pete?"

"Stupid idiot," I said. "That's the worst kind, I've heard."

I could see Warthog thinking. A long minute passed, and he said: "I'll accept the offer to resign if you let me announce I'm retiring for reasons of poor health. I do have a bad hip."

"We can do that," Roy said.

Warthog suddenly developed a limp and hobbled out of the room with his head held high.

When he was gone, I said to Roy, "I'll say this for him. He never cheated enough to get us on probation . . . just enough to get us investigated."

"You're right," Roy said with a nod. "He ran a clean program."

TEN

HOW WE wound up in the Big 10 borders on a saga. It happened four years ago in the midst of the Great Regurgitation, as the press called it. That was when CSN, the college sports television network, bought the rights to living, dying, breathing, eating, regularity, and major college football.

What this network did was money-whip the NCAA into becoming the NFL of college football.

There was already a small club of elite conferences that made up the Bowl Championship Series—the Big 10, SEC, Pac-12, ACC, and Big 12, plus independent Notre Dame, it goes without saying.

But CSN called on the elites to expand to eighty teams, which would mean more TV markets and more sponsors, and more money for the schools involved. The elites were told to expand into five sixteen-team conferences, and in return they'd share in a tidy $3.3 billion over fifteen years.

You could look at it like this: a football program at one single school out of the eighty would receive $47 million a year if it never even won a game, and if a school could win the national championship, it would collect up to $120 million.

If you asked me, it was an open invitation for schools to cheat—and for the NCAA to suddenly go blind. To keep its hand in, the NCAA would punish some school you'd never heard of for doing something nobody understood to reassure the public of its purity.

Overnight there was a scramble by the top conferences to grab more teams, and I was afraid Western Ohio would be left out. I felt like my job was hinging on me getting us into the Big 10.

I was losing my appetite worrying about us being included. In the evenings at home I'd find myself staring into space. Glenda was basically irritated that I didn't care to watch a golf tournament on TV with her.

The Big 10 needed two schools to reach sixteen. We felt Notre Dame would be one of them but the Irish surprised the world by going to the ACC. This was good. It put us in contention with other Big 10 candidates, such as Western Michigan, Miami of Ohio, Northern Illinois, UConn, and Temple, to name five.

Along with my appearing before a gathering of Big 10 athletic directors with an easel, a pointer, and a video presentation, I tried to lower the odds on our chances by doing some backroom work.

I confess I was prepared to commit perjury, theft, or robbery if it would help us join the ranks of Ohio State, Michigan, Iowa, Michigan State, Wisconsin, and the rest of the biggies. One thing I did was arm Rita Jo, Mike Hodges, and Rick Adams with cash and plastic and send them off to plant seeds in the right places. The right places were wherever they traveled to meet and entertain friendly sportswriters, sportscasters, ADs, assistant ADs, and coaches. They were to spread rumors about the schools we presumed to be our rivals.

Rita Jo said to a sportswriter in Minnesota, "I've heard from a reliable source that the faculty rep at Northern Illinois enjoys dressing up like Cleopatra and spends his weekends floating on a barge down the Kishwaukee River."

Mike Hodges whispered to a Wisconsin assistant football coach, "Did you hear about Western Michigan's deputy AD? He poisoned his neighbor's border collie. Think about that. The sumbitch killed Lassie."

Rick Adams dropped this on the assistant basketball coach at Michigan: "I don't like passing this on, but you might want to look deeper into the background of Miami of Ohio's defensive coordinator. He has a deep tan and speaks with an accent. I don't know about you, but that says Taliban to me."

Rita Jo caught the Iowa AD's attention when she said, "Have you heard about the faculty rep at Temple? She was hired because she claimed to be an African-American from Cleveland and a cousin of LeBron James. But it's soon to come out that she's white as a pillow case, she comes from Muskogee, Oklahoma, and played the dobro in an all-girl Western band."

Other things helped. We qualified as a "research institution." We have a fine law school. In the world of academics, our tenured faculty is respected, doubtlessly due to the fact that we have so many ex-hippie scum among our tenured professors.

Admittedly, I was moved when the call came from the commissioner of the conference, Russ Vance, telling me we'd been officially accepted.

"Welcome to the club, good buddy," he said.

A tear welled up and I couldn't speak for a minute.

All I could do was thank him for the good news, and thank the Lord for moving us into the high-rent district.

Our selection may have been as shocking as the Big 10 also inviting the University of Chicago to become the other selection. Chicago had been a charter member but quit football in 1940, having been overrun by eggheads. But they allowed themselves to be bought by CSN. The eggheads thought it over and concluded that it was smarter to stop inventing atom bombs and go for the television money.

■ ■ ■

THINGS HAPPENED elsewhere during the Great Regurgitation. The Atlantic Coast Conference, after kicking Louisville out to make room for Notre Dame, added Army and Navy to their North Carolinas and Clemsons, and called it patriotism.

The Big 12 was forced to find six new members. Thus the Oklahoma Sooners, Texas Longhorns, TCUs, and Texas Techs rescued Louisville and sent out a search party that brought in BYU, Cincinnati, Memphis, UConn, and Houston.

The Pac-12 invited Boise State, San Diego State, Nevada U., and the University of Hawaii—splendid choice for recruiting purposes—to join the Southern Californias, Stanfords, Cals, and UCLAs.

The SEC, already a powerhouse with members like Alabama, Auburn, LSU, Florida, and Georgia, had it easy. They only needed two more teams to beat every year like Kentucky and Vanderbilt, so they chose Tulane and South Florida. Two pleasant road trips to New Orleans and St. Petersburg, Florida.

When the dust cleared, there were fifty schools that thought they played major college football but no longer did. Predictably this led to a firestorm. Educators cussed and cried. Some screamed it was a plot against the black athlete. Others screamed it was a plot against the gay athlete. Still others screamed it was a plot against family values.

Lawsuits were threatened, some were filed. Daily newspapers, the ones that were still breathing, raved and blustered, then went back to printing government press releases and calling it reporting.

A group of U.S. senators yelled that they were going to repair the damage as soon as they returned to D.C., but when they returned they found themselves too busy to do anything but work on being re-elected, their main job. There were demonstrations on most of the campuses of the schools that were left out of the reshuffling. The networks reveled in covering the ones that led to fistfights and gunfire.

In the end, nothing happened to stop what the NCAA and CSN called progress. Dr. Byron Sanders, president of the NCAA, tried to put a happy face on the expansion. He traveled the country and made speeches about how the disappointed schools should be relieved to be out of the "arms race."

Most administrators at the left-out schools translated the NCAA president's message to mean they could go back to playing football in their old garbage dump conferences if they wished, but otherwise they could shut the hell up and stay out of the nation's sports pages.

So it turned out that greed remained undefeated and untied—and I can't tell you how happy I was to become a part of it.

ELEVEN

SLIDING Western Ohio into the Big 10 made me a hero on the campus for a whole month, nabbed me a staggering salary bump, but wound up causing trouble at home. Roy Clapper's wife, Janice, and Eddie Ralph Stoddard's wife, Rochelle, the pillars of local society, had never treated Glenda as their equal until I scored the Big 10. That sent our gong climbing up the social scales.

It prompted Janice and Rochelle to invite Glenda to go with them on one of their monthly shopping trips to Troy, Michigan, a high-end suburb of Detroit, where lurked the splendors of Neiman Marcus and Saks Fifth Avenue where you can buy something that costs three times as much as it's worth.

It was close to a three-hour drive from Shackayooka to Troy, thus the ladies always made it a "fun journey" by hiring a limo and driver for the occasion and bringing along wine and cheese. Glenda resisted but I encouraged her to go. So she did. But unfortunately it resulted in us getting into a rodeo over it. Rodeo. An old expression Texans rarely use now since people everywhere have started saying it.

This ain't my first rodeo, Darlene.

Like that.

Glenda's trip report wasn't what I hoped for.

She spent the drive to Michigan listening to Janice and Rochelle talk about a hairdresser named Foy, and listened on the drive home to Janice and Rochelle talk about the difficulties of finding a housekeeper who spoke English.

Glenda said to me, "I can't believe we live three hours from a Neiman Marcus."

I said, "If we lived in Dallas, we'd still be three hours from a Neiman Marcus. I've been to Dallas on business. I've seen Dallas traffic up close and personal."

According to Glenda, the highlight of the first few hours in the stores was watching Janice and Rochelle buy assorted items for $5,000 and up. This was in the moments when a haughty sales lady wasn't staring at her as if she were a shoplifter who'd wandered in off the street.

In an effort to put the haughty sales lady in her place, Glenda set about proving she could hammer the plastic with all the vigor of Janice and Rochelle. She returned home with six shopping bags filled with purchases made out of cashmere, suede, fur, silk, and pure gold that totaled over $12,000.

And I'd made her do it. By myself. Alone.

"Are you satisfied?" she said. "I'm sick about the money."

I said, "We can afford it. You made me proud. You held your own in a tough league."

She said, "I'll never wear any of this crap."

I said, "So throw all of it in the garage with your twenty-five sets of golf clubs we've accumulated over the years."

Got a look, but no laugh.

I wasn't as understanding in another of our rodeos.

After getting us into the Big 10, I could never have guessed what Glenda's reaction would be. It was: "Great, now we can join the Augusta National!"

I said, "We can do *what*?"

She said, "They will love to have us in the club. You're a big-shot athletic director in a major conference, and I shoot in the low seventies consistently. They won't have to worry about slow play on my part."

I said, "Glenda, are you nuts? All we know about Augusta National is what we've seen on TV. We've never been to the Masters. I'm not sure I've ever flown over Augusta, Georgia."

She said, "It won't hurt to ask about joining."

I said, "It's a private club, Glenda. About as exclusive as you can be. You don't ask to join. That's one of the unspoken rules in life concerning private clubs. You have to be *invited* to join. You should remember how happy you were when we were invited to join Bent Oak after I became AD."

She said, "So find somebody to invite us."

I said, "Who should I start with, Jack Nicklaus?"

She said, "I'm pretty sure jokes won't do it."

I said, "Glenda, I've never met a soul in this town who's a member of Augusta National. I don't even know anybody who *knows* a member. Have you ever heard anyone at Bent Oak say they've played the Augusta National golf course as a guest? I guarantee you if that person existed, our butts would be worn out hearing about his round."

She said, "I want to join that club, damn it. I'm serious about this. I've dreamed my whole life about playing the Big Track. I'm counting on you to make this happen."

Off and on over the next two months she asked if I was making any progress on getting us invited to join.

I first stalled around, saying, "I've found a guy who knows a guy."

Later, I said, "The guy I found didn't know the right guy."

Ultimately I said, "I keep calling the club's main number to ask about acquiring an application to join, but nobody answers."

One day she said, "I don't see why a golf club in Augusta, Georgia, should be more exclusive than any other club. You'll have to explain that to me."

I said, "It just is."

She said, "That's your answer?"

I said, "I read one time that they turned down the Prince of Wales."

She said, "Well, who wouldn't? He was dumb enough to piss away a damn good job."

TWELVE

IT WAS a joke around the office that Rita Jo held the unofficial title of Co-director of Sports Information. Members of the sports media gravitated to her when they came around in need of product and content, and not just due to her looks. It was because L.M. "Lunch Meat" Duncan, our official Director of Sports Information, was a master at dodging questions on any subject and knowing absolutely nothing about anything, even if it was something that happened in Norway.

L.M. spent half his time hiding from Coach Tag and the coach's anger. The rest of his time was devoted to avoiding a comment on anything that might be sensitive or scandalous.

Whenever L.M. was missing from the campus, he could be found at the 7-Eleven two blocks away unwrapping a baloney and cheese sandwich, his favorite food group. Which was why I nicknamed him Lunch Meat some years ago.

He was a stocky little guy with a beer belly and turning bald. He called everybody "Coach," "Sheriff," or "Hoss" because he couldn't remember names. When a sportswriter would try to draw a response from him on anything regarding football or basketball injuries or promotions and demotions in the lineup, Lunch Meat's standard response was, "Hoss, that dog won't hunt."

I inherited Lunch Meat Duncan. Amos Alonzo Howell hired him before I arrived. They met at a Final Four when L.M. was working at Southern Tech, a school in Mosquito Lake, Florida, that had become the talk of the hoops world by crashing the Final Four. Lunch Meat nicknamed Southern Tech's lineup "the Fabulous Felons."

He'd said it as a joke to a writer for *Sports Illustrated*, who claimed it for himself, and the rest of the sports media ran with it.

Amos hired L.M. as an urgent replacement for Zip Connor, his longtime director of sports information. Amos had been forced to fire Zip Connor for scalping Big U. football tickets and inventing names of business associates he entertained in bars and restaurants.

Zip Connor's expense reports too often listed "Coach Red Prosciutto," sportswriter "Dippy Harris," and sportscaster "Boffo Savage" among his dinner guests. The school's bookkeepers got around to discovering that Zip was basically entertaining himself and local pals.

People who've kept up with Zip say he landed well. He divorced his wife and married a rich widow with a bulging portfolio. Today his friends say Zip never leaves his chair and cigar on the veranda of their twenty-seven-room oceanfront villa in Palm Beach, Florida.

Football season should have been Lunch Meat's best time of year—we were wallowing in bowl games and national rankings. But it became his worst time. One reason was that Coach Tag would fire him and rehire him once a week during football season.

The coach would read something in a newspaper he didn't like—a note about his team or a quote the coach had uttered but didn't recall—and he'd blame Lunch Meat for letting it happen.

In an effort to keep L.M. from suffering a nervous breakdown, I met with the coach two seasons back and asked him to try to go easier on his publicist. Coach Taggert explained that it was his way of keeping L.M. alert.

I said, "Coach, there's nobody here more loyal than Lunch Meat."

The coach said, "I want him to be as loyal to me as he is to his baloney and cheese sandwiches."

I said, "I've seen you eat one."

He said, "I was in a hurry. He thinks it's cuisine."

I said, "No, he's aware it's just a snack. His cuisine is olive loaf."

Coach Tag said, "Loyalty goes a long way with me. I hope he knows it."

I said, "He does, and I'd trust him over some of your assistant coaches."

The coach said, "I'm no dummy, Pete. I have a mole on my staff. I want to know if any of my assistants are second-guessing me to the press behind my back. You never know about those turds."

"You have a mole on your staff?" I said.

He said, "Yes, like you do on the board—and don't tell me you don't."

I said, "How can you be sure your mole isn't your back-stabber?"

He said, "Mole Number Two would tell me."

I said, "You have a mole watching your mole? Pardon me for saying so, Coach, but I believe you're about half-paranoid."

"You're damn right I am," he said.

■ ■ ■

LUNCH MEAT developed and refined many talents working for the football coach. Among them was his habit of dodging the coach if he heard him tromping down the hall toward his office, rushing to the bathroom before the coach approached, picking up the phone and pretending to be on an important call if the coach was nearby, and dropping a ballpoint pen or his mouse on the floor and crawling under his desk to look around as the coach stuck his head in the door.

L.M.'s terror-stricken caution has resulted in his sending out press releases that fell somewhat short of enlightening. Some of the heads on his press releases: **Cheetahs Practiced Offense and Defense Wednesday. Coach Tag Admits Purdue Melee a Tossup. Coach Tag Says Hay in Barn for Iowa Tilt.**

I never saw Lunch Meat more worried about his ability than when we went into the Big 10. He worried that he didn't know how he was going to handle the pressure of operating in "the big league." He was shaking at the thought of having sportswriters from the big cities—Chicago, Detroit, Milwaukee—swoop down and pepper him with questions that Coach Tag wouldn't want answered.

I smiled at him and said, "Lunch, you'll just have to learn to tap dance a little better now."

"God," he said, and put his head in his hands.

I said, "What you have to keep in mind about the big-city sportswriters is, they put their laptops on one leg at a time like everybody else."

He said, "I don't know about that, Hoss."

I said, "Some of them have talent, sure. But most of 'em are among America's finest point-missers. They got their jobs because somebody died and they happened to be standing there."

"Is that right?" he said.

I said, "When they come to town your main job is to see that they don't go hungry or thirsty. You can't spend too much on that. Take 'em to Emily's, the best steakhouse in town. But if they want to go to Reba's Paradise and fall in love, they'll have to come up with their own cheese for that pleasure."

He said, "Lordy, you won't find me going anywhere near Reba's. If Nelda found out about it, she'd carve me a new one before I could get my pants down."

I said, "When you hear football talk from the big-timers, keep in mind that they really don't know dook about the game, they just act like they do. When they throw around terms like Triple Flex and Pistol Option and Bubble Screen, just smile like you know what they mean. If they ask if Coach Taggert is gonna keep his Armageddon Defense, you say that's a conversation he'll need to have with his defensive coordinator. If somebody asks you if Coach Taggert is gonna stay with his Fed Ex Spread, what do you say?"

"I have no idea," he said.

I said, "You say, 'Hoss, I believe Coach Tag would divorce his wife before he'd divorce his Fed Ex Spread.'"

"That's great," he said.

Rita Jo made me a promise. When the new AD replaces me and brings in his own people, she'll find a job for Lunch Meat somewhere on the campus so he can keep his medical and dental.

THIRTEEN

THE CAST of thousands Coach Tag called his football staff included his three top recruiters—Chick Overstock, Hog Elliott, and Marv Booker. They were also the best storytellers on the subject of what goes on in the stressful world of blue-chip recruiting wars.

Their personal experiences in trying to sign the most-wanted athletes made for a day of entertainment when some of us relaxed in the coach's conference room to smoke a cigar, have a beer, and speak freely.

Chick Overstock, our offensive coordinator, came to us from the University of Houston, a place where they'd been throwing the football for about 3,000 years. He modernized our attack. Coach Tag had always fancied a passing attack but not like a rainstorm.

Chick turned us into a Hell from Above, Fire from the Sky, Bomber Group Strike Force, and that's why Chick did everything he could to recruit Cody Cahill, a most-wanted quarterback in East Texas.

Apart from being a fantastic all-around athlete, Cody Cahill had a rifle for an arm and could put the ball on the numbers of a receiver fifty yards down the field. But that wasn't all. Cody could outrun a pack of wild dogs and knock down an elephant if that's what it took to get him to the end zone.

The trouble was, every major college knew about Cody Cahill and was throwing steak dinners, bimbos, and savings accounts at him. But Coach Overstock kept after him, believing he had an edge in that his offense suited Cody's talents better than any other team and would best prepare him for the NFL.

Chick arranged to see Cody in private to find out what would sway him toward Western Ohio. They met for lunch at Bo and Donna's Bait & Sandwich Shop near a small man-made fishing lake in the woods of East Texas.

When Chick steered the conversation around to what it would take to bring Cody on board, the kid hemmed and hawed and eventually said he did have a yearning for a bright blue Mustang Shelby GT350.

A week later Chick met Cody again at Bo and Donna's and presented him with the bright blue Mustang. In return, Cody signed a piece of paper pledging to attend Western Ohio, and promised to sign and fax the national letter of intent to Chick on February 2, which was signing day. Chick, in a state of ecstasy, was driven away by the driver in the SUV he'd hired to follow him.

Chick Overstock spent the next several days feeling like he'd gotten away with stealing the Crown Jewels. He felt like it up until signing day, when Cody's letter of intent never arrived, and he couldn't reach Cody on the phone.

A day later he found out why. He picked up a copy of *USA Today* and saw Cody's big grin in a photo and read that he'd chosen the school where he could play football best and seek a degree in . . . *Astrophysics?*

Alabama.

After devoting a day to punching holes in the walls of his office, Chick hopped on a plane to Dallas, rented a car and drove

120 miles an hour to Cody's home in Gusher, Texas. He invited Cody out in the front yard for a talk.

"Astro fucking physics?" Chick said, trying to control his temper.

Cody said, "I'm sorry, Coach. They told me to say that. They made a real good pitch at the last minute. They were awfully persuasive."

Chick said, "I can imagine. Well, there's nothing left for me to do but pick up the keys to the car."

Cody said, "That car's mine, man. I love that car."

Chick said, "Are you joking?"

Cody said, "You gave me that car. I'm keepin' it."

Chick said, "My ass, you are! That goddamn car cost us $65,000! You gimme those keys or you're gonna find yourself in big trouble."

"Really?" Cody Cahill grinned. "Who you gonna tell?"

▪ ▪ ▪

LINWOOD Coffey weighed 238, stood six four, and had played fullback at Cedar Grove High in a suburb of Indianapolis. Hog Elliott, our linebacker coach, thought Linwood would make a wrecking ball of a linebacker. His future in the pros would be on defense. He could start as a freshman at linebacker for any team in the country. Linwood was a *man*.

Each time Hog visited Linwood he would treat him to lunch at Linwood's favorite restaurant, Fat Boy Subs, where Linwood ate the Yard Long which came with so many cold cuts and cheese slices it would make Lunch Meat Duncan run away from home.

Hog said he could tell the kid how to play defense real quick. It was simple.

Hog told Linwood to stare at him, read his lips, and he said clearly, "On defense, Linwood, when they snap the ball, *hit* somebody."

When it came down to negotiations, Linwood wanted two trucks. One for himself and one for his parents. He wanted a house for his parents along with a job for his daddy, but it would have to be a job where his daddy didn't have to say "Yes, sir," to nobody—his daddy was "all done with that shit."

Hog told Linwood that he could arrange the apartment for him, but he wasn't sure what he could work out for the parents.

"Apartment don't do it for me," Linwood said. "I'll be needin' a house with a big yard."

Hog said, "A big yard for what?"

Linwood said, "My five dogs and my wife and her two lard-ass kids."

Hog Elliott said trying to sign Linwood was the first time he'd run into that many deal-breakers with one recruit. Hog suggested that Linwood skip college and football altogether and apply for a job with Bekins Moving & Storage.

Baylor took him.

■ ■ ■

EVERY recruiter agreed that if there was ever a defensive end with "can't-miss" stamped on his forehead, it was Dowdy Basham at B.H. Brady High School ten miles northwest of Shreveport, Louisiana. Dowdy was a black kid, a giant mobile hulk.

Marv Booker, our defensive line coach, couldn't guess Dowdy's exact measurements but it looked to him like Shaq O'Neal had decided to take up football in a second life. Dowdy lived with his folks in a cabin on property owned by a rich man in Shreveport.

The rich man only used the main house five times a year to entertain business associates and free-spirited ladies.

The first two times Marv Booker tried to make contact with Dowdy Basham and do his pitch, he was forced to find a parking place in a cluster of rent cars belonging to recruiters from Alabama, LSU, Georgia, Texas, Ohio State, Florida State, Texas A&M, and Notre Dame.

Marv never saw Dowdy on his first three visits. He'd try to wait out the high rollers, but would become exhausted and hungry and give up.

To Marv's surprise, he showed up alone one day and was invited into the cabin by Dowdy's parents. Dowdy was off doing something somewhere—might even have gone to school—but he should return soon.

By way of hospitality, Dowdy's mama offered Marv a big comfortable leather chair in the living room while she and Dowdy's daddy sat on a sofa watching soaps on a large TV that a nice fellow from Ohio State gave them.

Marv kept his patience for two hours waiting for Dowdy to return. The only thing he had to occupy his time was trying to keep a brown and white dog of unknown breed from chewing on his shoes and socks.

When Dowdy eventually came in the house, Marv made up his mind not to offer him a scholarship even before he stood up to introduce himself. That's because Dowdy Basham glared at him and said: "You're in my chair, honk-ass."

FOURTEEN

TO TELL the truth, I'm a weary sumbitch.

I'm tired of smiling, talking to strangers, shaking hands, making speeches, telling lies, and mostly tired of going to meetings and listening to people babble about nothing. Glad to be hanging it up.

I'm cruising past fifty-five, creeping up on sixty, and while I've heard that the sixties are the new forties, all I can say is I must have missed that crucial seminar.

The old-time ADs had it sweet. They worked for the football coach only. They didn't have to worry about making people around them feel *needed*. They knew how to use their influence when it was necessary to get something done and use their power when they dealt with the chin-rubbing procrastinators.

They seldom worried about athletes falling into serious trouble. Sure, the football players in their day might have car wrecks, wind up in street fights, tear up a frat house for the fun of it, and constantly ask for loans, but those things were easily taken care of.

Freshmen were ineligible. Drugs were unheard of. The varsity studs could handle their cigarettes and whiskey. The only snap course was P.E. Everybody made their grades to stay eligible, and everybody graduated. I mean, all but the knuckleheads who were forced to drop out of school and marry the cheerleaders they knocked up, and then hope to find a job somewhere.

Marriage is no problem for young people today. First of all, they don't marry, they hook up. Some accidentally or ignorantly have babies, lateral the babies off to their parents to raise, and hook up again.

There's no mystery in sex anymore. Teenage girls dress half-naked and might as well hang signs around their necks that say, "Do Me Next." Love means never having to say anything you can text first.

Once upon a time you had to be in the United States Navy to wear a tattoo, but in this culture somebody started the rumor that they're required for social acceptance. In a single afternoon walking across our campus, I'd spot a dozen babes who'd qualify as all-stars if their arms and backs weren't covered in ink.

One day I stopped a very pretty but inked-up coed and told her that if I wanted to read "The Rime of the Ancient Mariner," I'd go to the library.

I look forward to the day when tattoo removal is a growth industry.

◼ ◼ ◼

WHEN THE old AD fooled around with the football schedule, he didn't care about anything but trying to pay the freight. Sign up a Southern Cal for a non-conference game, take your lumps, bank the coin.

In my early days here, my problem was to seek a balance. I had to maximize the income from marquee games and minimize the number of potential losses. If I scheduled a home-and-home contract with a "name" school I thought we could beat—say the Vanderbilt Intellectuals or the Cal-Berkeley Commies—I'd need to shove in a Southern Northern and hope the Southern Northerns didn't show up with a stockpile of outlaws that would embarrass us.

I endured that pain more than once.

Good example: The season I brought in Delta State from Swamp Fever, Mississippi. I'd scheduled the school thinking it would be a mild workout for our team. But Delta State came loaded with a swarm of animals who hadn't been any closer to a classroom than Lil's Bayou Lounge. They kicked our butts halfway to the Gulf of Mexico.

There were other things the old ADs were lucky to avoid. There were only four "minor" sports for them to be concerned with. Baseball, track, golf, and tennis. Those kids played for the sheer fun of it, the joy of competition.

Today's youth would think that such an era must pre-date Napoleon. Not that today's youth would know who Napoleon was. He might well be the drummer in some rock band I'd never heard of. For me, that could be any group since The Mamas & The Papas.

◼ ◼ ◼

THE NICEST part for the old AD was, he didn't have trouble-making faculty members coming around to complain about his hiring practices. Why weren't there more women and minorities in his department?

I've learned not to stay irritated too long when I'd hear about it from Dr. Keith Kurth, a bearded, pipe-smoking professor of Psychology, and Dr. Edith Lawson, a foolish professor of Modern Language, or Political Dipshit Correctness, as it's known to me and sensible people.

I wasn't in the best of moods the day they came in my office yet again to discuss what Dr. Kurth called my "unfortunate situation" and Dr. Lawson called my "festering disease."

I said, "You know what, people? If this department was up to the brim with nothing but women and minorities in good jobs, you two would waltz in here and ask why I hadn't gone to the Congo and hired any pygmies."

Dr. Kurth said, "You, sir, have uttered an uncomfortable remark."

Dr. Lawson, chin lifted, rigid in her stance, said, "Mr. Wallace, you are a diversity-challenged embarrassment to this university."

I looked down at the paperwork on my desk, and said, "Fine. Report me to the principal's office."

They harrumphed out the door.

A day later I was summoned to see Chancellor Carpenter. I figured I was going to hear a lecture on my lackluster skills at dealing with faculty members.

I took a chair in the chancellor's outer office and waited twenty minutes to see him. I spent the time chatting with his secretary Dolores Winters, a gracious, appealing lady in her fifties with whom he'd been having an affair for three years. Everyone in town knew about their affair except Bernice Carpenter, the chancellor's ungracious, unappealing wife.

The chancellor was tied up with a newly discovered alum. Young guy named Tony Accosi, Dolores said. Tony had become new-rich arrogant and wanted to make a big donation to the school in person.

He was originally from Newark, New Jersey, but now lived in Rancho Santa Fe, California, and had boasted to Dolores that his property included a thirty-two-car garage, landing strip, and Formula One track. I didn't have to ask if he managed a hedge fund.

As Tony emerged from the chancellor's office I was dazzled by his tan and chest jewelry. He said, "Great day, huh—am I right, or am I Al Pacino?"

I dredged up a smile.

Dr. Carpenter was in his shirtsleeves with his tie loosened and chuckling as he doctored a glass of scotch rocks and removed a letter from between his teeth and waved it at me.

"Ten big ones, baby," he said, plopping down in the chair behind his huge desk. "The computers are talking to each other as we speak."

I asked, "What are the computers saying?"

He said, "They're saying ten million dollars. Ours is laughing out loud."

I said, "Ten million, uh? It sounds like we'll have to put his name on some building around here."

The chancellor said, "Maybe the business school—why not?"

Then he looked at me and said, "Now, Pete . . . *pygmies?*"

And broke into uncontrollable laughter.

My kind of chancellor.

FIFTEEN

I'D BE surprised to meet an athletic director who'd never dealt with a Booster Club Pest, as he's known around this bureau. We ADs swap stories at meetings and conventions about this type of fan.

The Booster Club Pest is loyal and means well but give him a chance and he'll turn into an all-conference Time Bandit. You have to find a way to distance him from the football program without insulting him, or, to take it a step further, having him shot.

We had a dandy around here for four years. Rusty Cameron. Rusty and his wife Courtney had gone to the Big U. in the Eighties, and had never gotten over it. Rusty had been a cheerleader and Courtney a Cheetah Girl. Their daughter, now a teenager, was named, in a jarring upset, Cheetah.

Rusty inherited his daddy's We-Got-'Em convenience store, expanded it to forty locations around the state, and did well enough to devote himself full-time to climbing the Cheetah Club social ladder until he was elected to a four-year term as the president.

When he became president of the boosters he and his wife started showing up in nothing but the school's orange and tan colors. Rusty was particularly fond of his orange suit, orange cowboy hat, and specially-made orange leather cowboy boots. Rusty saw it as his duty to attend every football practice and keep up to date on which high school players our coaches were trying to recruit. He'd spend much of his time at practices sidling up to Coach Taggert and whispering, "I hear we're close on the tight end in Chillicothe. What do you think?"

Coach Tag lost it one day at practice. He said to Rusty, "Will you get the hell away from me and my team? Do something. Go have a Tropicana."

Rusty dissolved into the background. He was a team player.

■ ■ ■

GRADES were something else the old ADs never had to bother with. I refer to the APRs, the academic progress rates, and the GPAs, the grade point averages. It was up to me to see that the football or basketball players didn't fall too far behind in their grades. We could be barred from post-season play, which meant we'd take a major financial hit on the budget.

If I decided to force a kid to transfer—for his own good, I liked to say—how did it affect the GPAs? If it was a smart kid with good grades, even though he couldn't tackle a wobbling drunk in a hallway, I might have to tell the coach to keep him. But if the kid had failing grades and he transferred in poor academic standing, that would count against the APRs.

Sometimes I'd have to make an athlete stay another semester to raise his grades, or I would have to employ the time-honored method a prominent Southern university invented many years ago—I wouldn't want to name names—which was hire somebody to do it for him. The big problem of dealing with scholar-athletes is that most of them think the APR and GPA are airline terminals named for dead presidents.

I did have one thing in common with the old-time athletic directors. They understood that the big financial contributors and the longtime season-ticket holders for football believed that only through their own blood, sweat, and tears had the football program risen to the heights it achieved.

What this means is, the big contributor and the longtime season-ticket holder need to be puppy-licked at every opportunity.

It's an accepted fact that four big contributors can fire a coach, three can fire an athletic director, two can fire a chancellor, and one *really big* contributor can fire everybody on the campus and rename the university after his son who'd never picked up anything heavier than the keys to a Corvette.

The big contributor is not as lenient as the season-ticket holder. Hobart (Hobo) Atkins is a classic example around the Big U.

Like most big contributors, Hobo came along as the program began to improve. He hopped on us like me on a tall glass of ice tea on a hot summer day. He started following the Cheetahs to bowl games, and decided that with his support we were going to become Notre Dame or Oklahoma and our empire would rule as long as he was alive, or we didn't suffer two losing seasons in a row.

Hobo Atkins is a hometown guy who says nobody remembers him from Walters High because he wasn't a football player or a cheerleader and he couldn't get a date with any girl in school who wasn't too fat or too skinny or didn't talk too much for her own good.

I hold people like Hobo in awe. He's one of those guys who goes off and becomes rich in mysterious ways you can't understand because he knows something about money the rest of us haven't figured out yet.

He's firmly entrenched among the power brokers at the Town Club. Already has his own chair in the smoking room.

I have taken Hobo's word that he owns the three ranches in Wyoming, Idaho, and Canada, the chalet in Jackson Hole, the apartment in London, and the two private jets he travels in—the Global 5000 and the Citation X.

Another of his possessions is his fourth wife, Melody, a Hooters girl he met in Houston on a trip when he tried to buy NASA. Hobo turned Melody over to "his people" and they transformed her into a fashionable lady with a regal manner. Her makeover works at social functions until Melody opens her mouth and says, "Ain't this the shits?"

We handle a big contributor like Hobo delicately. We drape him in bowl game rings, championship rings, game balls, autographed jerseys and helmets, and framed photos of him with various personalities, including the current Miss America, Frieda von Bremen, a Miss Ohio who had been a student at the Big U. for fifteen minutes, and who is rumored to be a candidate for Hobo's fifth wife.

■ ■ ■

THE DEVOUT season-ticket holder is easier to please. He's a person who's been around forever, sitting in the same stadium seat, parking in the same spot, tailgating with the same crowd. He was there during the bad years, but never complained about losing, only when somebody forgot to bring what they were assigned to bring to his tailgate, such as cheeses of the world.

The season-ticket holder is loyal to the point of embarrassment. He never sees the Cheetahs lose a game. He does see us get screwed out of winning, and bad-lucked out of winning. He blames hot weather for losses as often as he blames cold weather for losses. Injuries frequently do it. Assistant coaches can be held responsible.

Back in our dog days, he could explain how one bad bounce of the football was so demoralizing, it made the difference in a 46-0 loss to Bowling Green.

What we do with this faithful fan is pound him with plaques. If he's been around long enough, it's a cinch he's been awarded the Distinguished Alumni Award, the Cheetah Club's Man of the Year Award, the Cheetah Club's Man of the Decade Award, the Lettermen's Association Most Faithful Fan Award, Western Ohio University's Sustainer of the Year Award, the Western Ohio University's Hall of Excellence Award, the Royal Orange & Tan Award, the Big Cat 'O Fame Award, and if he lived a little longer he would qualify for some other awards Rita Jo hadn't thought up yet.

It is hilariously said around my office that if you want a plaque, put on an orange shirt and tan jacket and go stand on a street corner—the AD will be along any minute to make a presentation.

SIXTEEN

THERE'S one more thing the ADs of bygone years never had to worry about. Personal problems.

When did athletes become so fragile? Personal problems used to be for parents and preachers to take care of. The athlete understood this, and if he didn't understand it, some old iron-pants, foul-mouthed coach ran him up and down the stadium steps until he *did* understand it—or quit football and started taking piano lessons.

I sometimes thought we'd been invaded by athletes with personal problems. I had this notion that any athlete today who didn't have a personal problem would watch TV or search the Net until he found somebody who'd suggest one to him.

But there were those who couldn't get out of their own way. Bubba Rutherford was one. He was the six-foot-six, 337-pound defensive end who was arrested for domestic violence.

Bubba's live-in girlfriend—Snookie—accused him of throwing her down two flights of stairs in their apartment building. She suffered multiple bruises and a broken rib. Bubba's version differed. He said they were arguing about money and it evolved into pushing and shoving, and his hand got caught in her lovely long hair, and he couldn't get his hand loose, and it was her hair that pulled them both down the stairs.

It was up to me to persuade Snookie and her parents not to file assault charges, which they didn't. Rita Jo reacted with a grin, and said, "I knew money would help them come to their senses." I said, "What money?"

Coach Tag was furious with Bubba and threatened to kick him off the squad, but he thought it over in a calmer frame of mind and concluded that every young man who makes a big mistake deserves a second chance. Bubba accounted for twelve unassisted tackles and four sacks the following Saturday against Michigan State.

Coach Tag was gracious enough to give me credit for dealing with two other athletes who were in danger of developing personal problems.

One was Riley "Farm Dog" Holt. He was our unanimous two-time All-America linebacker and Butkus Award winner. He came to us from Hill Country Junior College in Texas, where he learned to eat with silverware.

That's where he earned his nickname. His coach at Hill Country, J.T. Hubbard, gave it to him. J.T. said the big, tough, quick, and agile Riley Holt could chase a ball-carrier up a tree faster than his best farm dog.

Coach Tag thought the problem with Riley was, he hated opponents too much. He didn't just want to win, he wanted to do bodily harm. His minimum goal was to cause two carry-outs and four limp-offs in every game.

In the middle of Riley's first All-America season, Coach Tag worried that Riley was psychotic enough to injure an opposing player permanently. Riley liked to stand over a guy he'd left whimpering on the ground and say, "Hurts, don't it?" The coach didn't want to take anything away from his intensity, so he sent Riley to me so I could look around in his head.

I started off with Farm Dog by saying, "You're the best linebacker I've ever seen on a football field, but do you really hate your opponents?"

He said, "Supposed to, ain't you?"

I said, "I guess so, if you feel it's in conjunction with school spirit."

He said, "Fuck 'em."

I said, "Fuck 'em? You feel that in your heart, do you?"

He said, "Yeah, in my heart, my ass, and ever place else that counts."

I said, "Would you care to explain why?"

He said, "They shouldn't have gone to that school."

"Uh huh," I said with a nod.

He said, "When I hit a motherfucker, I want him to know he's been hit and remembers who fuckin' did it."

I said, "Farm Dog, I'm thinking somebody somewhere along the way may have given you a confusing idea of sportsmanship."

"Sportsmanship's ass," he said. "Man catches a pass in my zone, I'll spear him in the spine with my hat. Hope he don't get up. I'll step on his arm in a pileup too. Mash down on a knee, see if I can hear a click. I've heard my share of clicks."

"I'm sure you have," I said. "Do you partake in conversations with our rivals during a game?"

He said, "Do I what?"

I said, "Talk to your opponents in a game?"

He said, "Yeah, if I take a hard hit, I say, 'Good lick, brother.' That's football."

"Good," I said. "I'm pleased to hear it."

He said, "But when I stop a sweep, I tell the motherfucker if he tries to run that sweep on me again, I'm gonna send his fag ass out of the stadium in a body bag or an ambulance, whichever shows up first."

"Uh huh," I said again.

He said, "We 'bout done with this shit, Mr. Wallace?"

His maniacal gaze told me we were.

■ ■ ■

COACH Tag's other athlete with a personal problem was a highly skilled pass receiver. Kid named Bobby "Brains" Terrell.

Bobby had watched a TV documentary about athletes who'd won the Olympic decathlon and decided he didn't want to play football anymore. He told Coach Taggert he wanted to switch to track and field and concentrate on the decathlon and win the Olympic gold medal and become "the world's greatest athlete" and get rich and see his picture on a Wheaties box.

Brains Terrell was one of those recruits we'd taken a chance on when no other college wanted him. He was a product of a miserable neighborhood in Cleveland. He'd learned nothing in his public schools because his teachers were usually on strike.

He'd once been in a gang when he was fourteen. He told Coach Taggert that being in the gang was where he learned to catch things with both hands. The older gang members would rob an electronics store in broad daylight and throw items out the door for him to catch and run away with. Cell phones, tape recorders, headsets, batteries.

But he knew he was good at sports. He liked to play football, baseball, and basketball better than he liked stealing things. The other thing was, he had instinctively known that, unlike his two older brothers, he didn't want to be dead by the time he was eighteen, victim of a gang war.

When I called Bobby "Brains" Terrell in for a sit-down, the first thing I said was, "Do you prefer to be called Bobby or Brains? How'd you acquire that name anyway?"

He said, "I been called Brains a long time. My high school coach gave me the name in a workout. I was a running back to start with. I kept missing the hole on an off-tackle play in scrimmage. It never was a big hole. It wasn't my fault. But he called me Brains. My teammates picked up on it. 'Yeah, he Brains,' they hollered. I been Brains ever since."

I said, "Does the nickname bother you?"

He shrugged, and said, "Whatever happen, happen."

I repeated that with a laugh. "*Whatever happen, happen?* That's mine now. I'm claiming it."

He said, "You got anything to drink in here?"

I pointed to the fridge and said, "Help yourself."

When he sat back down with a can of Coke, I said, "Brains, I'm not sure you understand what the decathlon is."

He said, "Runnin', jumpin', throwin' things."

I said, "Let me explain more about it to you. Take the four track events. The one-hundred-meter dash, one hundred and ten hurdles, four-hundred-meter dash, and fifteen-hundred-meter run. Have you ever been to New York City, Brains?"

He said, "Not really."

I said, "*Not really?* Does that mean you've only been there in your mind? You'll have to explain that, if it's not a bother."

He said, "Didn't we fly over it when we went up to play Army?"

I said, "You're right, we did."

"Looks tall," he said. "People get dizzy living that high up?"

I said, "It's a tall city. Most people live in the shorter buildings."

"I sure would," he said.

I said, "Most of the people work in the tall ones. Now listen. If you ever go there in person, like on the ground, you're going to see people everywhere—men, women, kids—who can outrun you in every decathlon event, and they'll only be trying to catch a taxi."

He squinted at me.

I said, "Let's talk about the field events—high jump, long jump, pole vault. If you want to see an average man in a business suit holding a briefcase out-jump and out-vault you? Tell him you're with the Internal Revenue Service."

Brains looked as if he thought he should laugh.

I said, "How about the other field events? You want to know who can throw an armchair further than a decathlete can throw a shot put, discus, or javelin? A pissed-off girlfriend."

"I hear that," he said.

"Here's the point I'm making," I said. "The decathlon athlete isn't good enough to win *any* of those events against world-class specialists. What it comes down to is, the athlete who wins the Olympic decathlon is *not* the world's greatest athlete. He's the world's most *ordinary* athlete."

He said, "Really?"

I said, "Do what you're best at, Brains. Stick to football."

He's with the Dolphins now.

SEVENTEEN

IN THE history of personal problems, it would be impossible to top the one that involved the most talented quarterback in the history of Western Ohio football. What happened on the roof of Old Ad that night could have resulted in grave damage to the university if it hadn't been for a God-fearing, quick-thinking individual—namely me.

I shared the details of the incident with Rita Jo and Coach Taggert. They deserved to be prepared in case the more humorless educators on our faculty would hear about it and try to turn it into an academic crisis.

The phone rang at 9:30 on that Sunday evening. I was home watching Masterpiece on public TV. Like most of America, Glenda found herself hypnotized each week by a particular series she would only miss if our house caught on fire. To me, however, it was just another of those British dramas where people take long walks.

A campus security guard called to inform me that one of our football players was standing on top of the administration building either drunk or doped up—it was hard to say which.

The guard said, "I think I should tell you he's stark naked and holding what looks like a big old knife."

I said, "Is this a joke? Who is this?"

He said, "My name is Cecil H. Padgett . . . Dead-Eye Security . . . Badge 346. No, it's not a joke, Mr. Wallace. There's one other thing—I'm fairly sure it's our quarterback."

"You're not serious," I said.

He said, "Yes, sir, I'm afraid I am."

I said, "Let me see if I have this straight, Cecil. You're telling me the naked man with a knife standing on top of Old Ad is Kenny 'Golden Kid' Sealy from Oceanside, California, our golden-haired, poster-boy quarterback and Heisman Trophy candidate. That's what I'm hearing?"

The security guard said, "Yes, sir, it's Kenny up there. I'm looking right at him."

"What is he doing this minute?" I said.

The guard said, "A while ago he was talking to the solar system, but right now he appears to be talking to his dick."

"I'll be right there," I said.

■ ■ ■

I WAS STILL dressed. It took me only five minutes to drive to the campus. I parked in the lot behind Old Ad and walked around to the side of the building where the security guard was standing— and where I could see our Heisman Trophy candidate on the roof.

"Is that you up there, Kenny?" I hollered.

He called back down, "Yeah, it's me, Pete. Me and Raymond."

I didn't bother to ask who Raymond was. I raced into the building, ran up the three flights of stairs to the top floor, scaled the ladder that led to the push-up door that opened onto the roof. I worked my way around the air-conditioning and heating units and the bathroom vents and found Kenny.

I sat down heavily, gasped for breath, and said, "What's going on, Kenny? I'd appreciate knowing before I pass out."

He said, "I'm tryin' to decide what to do about Raymond."

I said, "Who the hell is Raymond?"

Kenny glanced down at his penis, and said, "Raymond my binness."

I said, "Kenny, I have to tell you, I've heard a man's binness called Wilber . . . Johnson . . . Big George . . . Leroy . . . Uncle Billy . . . Buster . . . even Old Percy when my wife and I were on vacation in England, but I've never been introduced to a Raymond."

I was pleased to notice that Raymond was on idle.

I asked, "How'd you come up with that name, Kenny?"

Kenny said, "Raymond's named for a dog I had when I was a kid. He fucked everything in the neighborhood. What he didn't fuck, he killed. He was a Chow dog."

I said, "They say your Chows can be testy. Whatever happened to Raymond?"

Kenny said, "A policeman shot him. Raymond was trying to chew through a knothole fence so he could get after a girl sunbathing in her backyard."

I said, "Kenny, do you have any clothes with you?"

He said, "My jeans and T-shirt and flip-flops are over there in a pile."

I said. "I've always had trouble trying to have a conversation with a naked man. Or a naked woman, as far as that goes. You want to do me a favor and put your clothes on?"

I watched him slip into his duds.

I said, "I don't like to see you with that knife up here either, Kenny."

He said, "I came up here to cut Raymond off my body. Get him out of my life. Raymond's making me fuck so much, I'm likely to be too tired to play football next season."

"Kenny," I said, "you haven't been taking those hard-on pills, have you? Like in the TV commercials? Where the gray-haired guy and his wife go sailing and dancing under the stars, then the wife looks like she can't wait to get to their hotel room so the old boy can bang her like a screen door in a Texas tornado?"

Kenny said, "Raymond don't need anything to make him horny. Raymond fuck this roof if I chisel a hole in it."

I said, "Listen to me, Kenny. There's medication to take care of Raymond. And if you were to get rid of Raymond, I promise that you will badly miss him the rest of your natural life."

He said, "Raymond's good most of the time. It's lately he's been acting, you know, kind of unmanageable."

I was quiet for a moment, thinking this was some jackpot I'm in.

Then I said, "What are you on, Kenny? I know you're on something. Did you substance abuse yourself, or did somebody substance abuse *you*?"

He said, "Pete, I was celebrating the end of spring training. I was in a bevy of contessas over at Honcho Jimmy's on the Drag. We were throwing down beers and Fireball shots. I can normally handle that, but maybe one of the second team contessas slipped me a who-gives-a-shit pill, thinking I'd ignore my preferences in contessas and she'd get lucky."

I said, "See, Kenny, I can take the blame for part of your problem. I must have never stressed to you in strong enough terms that throwing down beers and Fireball shots at Honcho Jimmy's on the Drag doesn't necessarily present the best image for our university."

He said, "Even in the off-season?"

I sighed. "Uh-huh. Even in the off-season."

He said, "Raymond was liking all the contessas. I could tell. He wouldn't have culled any of 'em."

I said, "Golden Kid, you have to straighten yourself out and realize something. You can put the Big U. on your shoulders next season and take us to the playoffs. You're capable of throwing thirty-five, forty touchdown passes next season. You're guaranteed to be a first-round draft choice in the NFL. You'll sign a five-year contract for—hell, I'm guessing—maybe fifteen million before you take your first snap."

He said, "Whoa, you sure about that amount?"

I said, "I'll find you an honest agent. Not one of those thieves who only wants your money. But you are NOT gonna see any money if you let yourself turn into a no-count, whiskey-drunk, dope-sick lame-brain. You hear what I'm saying, Kenny, or am I talking to Raymond?"

He grinned.

I said, "I'm beyond serious, Kenny."

He said, "I hear you, Pete. I'm starting to feel better. My mind's coming back. What do you want me to do?"

I said, "I guess the first thing I'd like to see you do tonight is not cut off your dick."

He slid the knife over to me.

I said, "Good move, Kenny. Now we'll keep tonight between you and me. How's that sound? I know you don't want to let your team down."

He said, "Pete, I don't want anything to come between me and my team. I love my teammates. I love 'em like I love most of my family."

I said, "What's wrong with the part of the family you don't love?"

He said, "Aw, I have an older brother and sister who are kind of sorry. You know. Like some people are just sorry folks?"

"What do they do?" I asked.

"That's the thing," he said. "They don't do anything. My brother was a disc jockey in a warehouse for a while. My sister was a pole dancer. But they quit and moved back home. Now they lay around stoned day and night. If my folks kicked 'em out of the house, they'd flop down in the yard and stay there, no matter how many times you jabbed 'em with a rake or something."

I said, "My daddy always said he liked to help people who *can't* help themselves, but he'd piss on those who *won't* help themselves. Your folks ever try kicking dirt over your brother and sister?"

He said, "They'd think it was a blanket."

I sighed and said, "Sometimes you have to shoot your own dog."

Kenny said, "Pete, I swear I'm done screwing around till after the season. I don't care how many contessas try to kidnap me."

We left the building. I took two hundred-dollar bills out of my money clip and handed them to Cecil H. Padgett, Badge 346, and said, "Anything happen around here tonight?"

The security guard said, "Nothing I recall, Mr. Wallace."

"You're a good man, Cecil," I said.

We walked over to Krueger's All-Night Drug on the Drag, an institution. More of a hangout than the Student Union. It has good food, an old-fashioned soda fountain, and booths. We drank coffee and talked a while longer. Afterward, I walked him home the three blocks to the apartment he shared with Omar Mustafa, formerly Johnny Gates, his most reliable passing target.

Kenny's Porsche and Mustafa's Jaguar were parked in the driveway. I've never wanted to know where those vehicles came from.

We kept the incident covered up. Coach Tag said he should have kicked the stupid shithead off the team, but he didn't want to look for another coaching job.

Kenny was the quarterback who led us to our 12-1 season and that lick we put on Auburn in the Aunt Jemima Buttermilk Pancake Mix Sugar Bowl.

Kenny was a consensus All-American, won the Maxwell and Camp awards, but didn't win the Heisman, which was a crime. He finished second to an overrated Nebraska quarterback who played on a team that lost three games, and whose stats wouldn't have made a pimple on Kenny's butt. It's a shame so many morons are allowed to vote on that award.

I still predict that Kenny "Golden Kid" Sealy will lead the Dallas Cowboys to their greatest seasons—if he can stay out of rehab.

Rita Jo said, "I'm just happy to know Raymond survived and will live to have romance in his life again."

EIGHTEEN

MY DEPUTY called at noon that day. She was eager to know if I'd heard anything from my moles among the trustees.

I said, "You don't have a mole on the board. I'm shocked."

Rita Jo said, "I used to. He went back to his wife."

I said, "There's no end to sad stories in this world."

She said, "I assume Her Ladyship is at the club today."

I said, "She was gone when I got up. Early tee time, is my guess."

She said, "What if I go to Krueger's and bring you lunch? Hot pastrami on toasted rye with sauerkraut, cheese, and Thousand Island."

"One of my faves," I said, "but I brought peanut butter and peach jelly on light bread from home."

"Skippy and Smuckers to the rescue again," she said. "I should stop by for a while anyhow. I know you can use company."

I said, "Your concern is appreciated, babe. I'm good. I'm having fun with the voice recorder. You know I'll holler when I hear something."

She said, "You sure? I could sit on your lap. We could play doctor and nurse."

She was howling with laughter as she clicked off.

NINETEEN

AN ATHLETIC director could never say this in public, but in idle hours I'd occasionally think of ways for a football official, the guy with a yellow flag—a zebra—to die in agonizing pain.

Mauled by a black bear on a family vacation with his wife and children watching? Strangled by a giant squid after accidentally falling overboard on a deep-sea fishing trip? Carved into small pieces by a crazed surgeon after going into the hospital for a simple hemorrhoidectomy?

Just joking.

I wouldn't intentionally wish any of that on a fellow human, even a zebra. Even the ones who cost us the national championship, although it might depend on how many martinis I'd had.

Two seasons ago we looked like the best team in the country throughout our regular schedule. We were ranked No. 1 for the last six weeks. We were 12-0, and behind Kenny "Golden Kid" Sealy we'd averaged 47 points a game, won each of them with ease, and wrapped up the Big 10's Western Division.

The Western Division was where the conference placed us when we entered the league. In there with Iowa, Wisconsin, Nebraska, Minnesota, and, as Rita Jo said, "Indiana and three other teams with no pulse."

That season we not only had Kenny Sealy going for us, we also had other weapons. We were blessed with our All-America pass receiver, Omar Mustafa, formerly Johnny Gates, and our two defensive All-Americans, Riley "Farm Dog" Holt and Bubba Rutherford. And there was our handy ramrod fullback, Leonard Leonard, or I should say Leonard "Typo" Leonard, as Lunch Meat Duncan wittily named him.

Coach Tag had recruited Leonard Leonard out of Uwchlan, Pennsylvania, a town apparently named by the worst speller among its settlers.

Typo was six two and 247. He wasn't a broken-field runner but he could move the pile. He was automatic for a first down on short yardage. If you wanted a concrete wall knocked down, he was your man. In the huddle, he'd say "Gimme foobaw," and go do it.

It was spellbinding to watch Typo eat the pre-game meal. He thought the bone on a steak was the best part. Crunched it up like chewing gum. He could have done real damage to a zebra's leg.

When we took on Michigan to settle the Big 10 title we were 14-point favorites and assured of a dry field. The game was played under the roof of Lucas Oil Stadium in Indianapolis, a neutral site.

While we were undefeated, Michigan had lost an early battle to Stanford, but the Wolverines won their other eleven games to take the Eastern Division over their main rivals, Ohio State and Michigan State.

In the buildup to the game, the national press convinced both schools that if it was close the Cheetahs and Wolverines would both be selected to participate in the four-team playoffs for the national championship. The semifinals were scheduled for the Orange Bowl, the championship game in the Rose Bowl.

I'm here to testify that no team ever absorbed a worse screwing than we did. We lost the nail-biter 55-52, but there was another number that told the true story. The number was twelve for 155. That's the outrageous number of penalties and yards the zebras called on us compared to the three puny motion penalties for five yards each they called on Michigan.

I wouldn't have minded losing to Michigan fairly. I'm an admirer of Michigan. Great helmets, rich history.

We were seated in a luxury suite. On the front row were Rita Jo and me, Roy Clapper, Chancellor Carpenter, Eddie Ralph Stoddard, and Hobo Atkins. The other ladies were on the row behind us—Glenda, Janice Clapper, Rochelle Stoddard, Dolores Winters, and Melody Atkins.

The suite was equipped with a well-stocked bar, snacks, a waiter, and two large TV sets on the walls. Comfort was our friend.

Rita Jo and Dolores Winters, the chancellor's lady friend, were more interested in the game than the other ladies. Melody spent the afternoon texting. Janice Clapper and Rochelle Stoddard chatted about shopping and their volunteer duties for local charities. Glenda devoted most of the day to playing a Jordan Spieth golf game on her iPad. Near the end of the first quarter it had become evident to Rita Jo and us gentlemen that the zebras were less concerned with calling the game honestly than they were with building up their secret accounts in the Caymans.

When the referee called holding on us for the second time to slow down what was looking like a scoring drive, Rita Jo leaped out of her seat and yelled down at the field: "Al Capone, I thought you were dead!"

It drew laughter from the menfolk.

Rita Jo headed for the bar, saying she was going to need fortification to put up with the zebras.

Glenda said to Rita Jo, "But it's only a game, right? I know I've heard that somewhere."

Rita Jo said, "The heck it is. It's what an old coach once said—I can't remember who. He said, 'A big football game is not a matter of life and death, it's more important than that.'"

I interrupted to say, "Duffy Daugherty said it, I think. Maybe not."

Glenda said, "God, I hope we can clear that up before the day's over."

Rita Jo laughed and said, "Damn it, Glenda, you know I hate it when somebody is funnier than me."

I said, "We're about to score, if anybody's interested."

The game became a track meet. It was something of a miracle that we managed to keep scoring regardless of the penalties called on us.

In her anguish over the zebras, Rita Jo renamed the umpire John Dillinger, the field judge John Gotti, and said Michael Corleone was in the replay booth. With two minutes left to play, we were trailing the Wolverines 48-45, but Kenny "Golden Kid" Sealy had one more great play in him. After driving us to Michigan's 30, he dropped back to pass, escaped a fierce rush, and couldn't find a receiver open, even Omar Mustafa, formerly Johnny Gates. So Kenny kept dashing this way and that, slipping tackles, and finally zig-zagged into the end zone for the touchdown. A highlight film in one play.

When that put us up 52 to 48 with less than a minute to play, I envisioned our fans dreaming of a lovely week in Miami Beach and calling Joe's Stone Crab for future dinner reservations.

But our lead only made the zebras work harder. After we kicked off, a roughing the passer penalty, a defensive holding penalty, and two interference calls managed to put Michigan on our goal line. From there, the Wolverine quarterback faked a hand-off, and scooted in for the winning touchdown.

I went down to the dressing room to commiserate with Coach Tag, his assistants, and some of the players. Everybody but the head coach was bitching about the robbery.

Even this time, Coach Tag refused to criticize the zebras. He never complained about an officiating crew.

He said, "I know it looked one-sided today, but we were responsible for some of it. You have to write it off. One day an officiating crew will win a big one for *us*."

That wasn't good enough for me. I wanted the sumbitches stuck on tree limbs where they'd be eaten by giraffes at the nearest zoo.

It was the two pass interference calls that were the real killers. Forget the fact that our defensive backs never came close to touching anybody. What I'll remember most is that the passes were so far over the heads of the Michigan receivers, Moses on top of Mount Sinai reaching up with both hands couldn't have caught them.

TWENTY

THE MEETINGS I was obligated to attend in line with my job often made me tired enough to lie down in the street and risk getting trampled to death by an onslaught of joggers, who, I dare say, wouldn't break stride until they keeled over from their heart attacks.

At first I used to go to twenty meetings a year, but I smartened up and reduced it to ten, which was plenty. Among them were the conference meetings, the NCAA meetings, the AD meetings, and the assorted committee meetings that would spring out of the other meetings.

The organizers offered up highly paid motivational speakers to entertain us. In the first five minutes of their lectures, I'd become about as attentive as your average Egyptian mummy.

I could hardly forget the year the organizers enlisted Bomber Colby to enrich our lives. He'd been an All-America quarterback at Penn State, but you would have no reason to remember him when he played for the Buffalo Bills. He never led them anywhere near a division title.

But to hear Bomber Colby tell it, he could have won as many Super Bowls as Terry Bradshaw, Joe Montana, and Tom Brady if he hadn't been saddled with an offensive line that couldn't block a group of old ladies, pass receivers with arthritic fingers, and one of the Three Stooges for a head coach.

Equally irritating was the female sideline reporter for CSN-TV, Angela DeAngelo. Her chirpy voice asking stupid questions on the air made me want to snatch the voice out of her throat and grind it into the floor with John Wayne's boot.

I'd already learned from watching Angela on TV that her idea of a penetrating question to a coach or a player was, "What does it mean to you that you've never had cancer?"

Not even the fine wine, flowing whiskey, and sumptuous buffets in the hospitality suites compensated for the agony perpetrated by the speakers.

After the first few years I softened the pain of the meetings by taking Rita Jo along. She would be in charge of listening and taking notes if anything important was said while I read a paperback mystery or cut class to take a stroll.

Rita Jo's presence made me instant friends with many of the ADs. I was the guy with the show-stopper in tow. When I first introduced Rita Jo as my deputy, I'd hear the proverbial, "Sure, Pete, where's your niece from?"

But they'd soon discover she was smarter than them.

At first I was inexperienced enough to let myself be trapped into serving on whatever committees my peers wanted me on. Those happened to be finance, marketing, scholarships, education reform, diversity employment, faculty involvement, and future planning.

Everybody but me filibustered in the meetings and the only thing resolved was that we should hold another meeting to discuss the issues in more detail. But I learned to become a skillful committee dodger.

Relief came when I was appointed a permanent member of the Football Rules & Officiating Committee. Here was a subject that would hold my interest and I could become vocal about.

Not that we had much influence on our football coaches. Today the coaches continue to make rules changes to justify the week they'd spend playing golf at a resort. This has resulted in the four worst rules ever perpetrated on college football—Targeting, Taunting, Excessive Celebration, and Block in the Back.

Taunting and targeting were part of the college football I played. If you went back in history and called penalties for excessive celebrations, you could change the result of a number of games that settled the national championship. And the only thing the block in the back does on punt and kickoff returns is make you look for the flag.

It amazes me that nobody sees the block in the back but the zebra. Particularly if the game's on TV.

"Honey, did you see me call back that ninety-yard touchdown run? It was a real heartbreaker, huh?"

Another concern for me is the replay guy upstairs. I would like to take the game out of the hands of this wizard. Half the time, what he sees is never what the rest of America sees. My suggestion in meetings was to give the coaches two challenges per half on a questionable call and be done with it.

The rest would be rub of the green, as in the game of golf, and as Glenda would say in a match to her opponent whose golf ball in the fairway had been carried off by a large bird.

TWENTY ONE

AS A dues-paying golf widow, I could readily testify that the officers of the Collegiate Athletic Directors Association knew what they were doing when it came to selecting resorts for the three biggest meetings of the year. Glenda never missed those trips, and became accustomed to staying in the finest hotels and playing famous golf courses.

The Pebble Beach Lodge was where she could play Pebble Beach and Spanish Bay. She twice tried to talk her way onto ultra-private Cypress Point on 17-Mile Drive but got laughed at—and almost arrested. She liked the Greenbrier where she played Old White and four other courses, and the Broadmoor where she played the Mountain course and two others, and she loved the Kahala Hotel in a suburb of Honolulu where she could play Waialae Country Club every day.

She would pay for a playing lesson with a teaching pro at Waialae, or the pro shop would arrange a game for her with a tourist gentleman whose wife might be recovering from the previous night's attack of the Mai Tais.

Staying at the Kahala enabled Glenda to enjoy doing something else when she wasn't donning her cleats. She would stroll around the swimming pool and strike up friendships with well-built, well-tanned Mainlanders who looked like movie stars.

On one trip when Rita Jo was along and a group of us were lounging around the pool, Rita Jo explained to Glenda that those guys weren't movie stars, they were valet parkers on their day off from other hotels and restaurants.

Rita Jo added, "A handsome valet parker isn't interested in you or me, Glenda. He's looking to scoop up a wealthy divorcee and live the rest of his life as a wasted fop."

Glenda said, "What is a *wasted fop*, Rita? I'm not as well-educated as you. I went to Flat Beach State."

Rita Jo said, "A waste of human tissue."

Glenda said, "Oh? Well, we'll have to keep a sharp eye out for that, won't we?"

Rita Jo rewarded her with a laugh.

◼ ◼ ◼

THESE trips were fine for Glenda's golf addiction, but not always fine in the evenings when we'd have dinner with other ADs and their wives and Glenda would down enough red wine to feel snappier than usual.

I'd find myself on the edge of my chair. Me and Tagamet.

One night after dinner on a trip when Rita Jo was with us, a fellow AD couldn't help but notice Glenda throwing out lines here and there, all of them from her repertoire of cynical humor. Misinterpreting her humor for rudeness, the AD pulled me aside to ask what had put Glenda in such a bad mood?

Rita Jo overheard the question and answered it.

"Ten thirty," she said.

I may have laughed too hard at that.

◼ ◼ ◼

I COULDN'T have guessed what Glenda thought her life would be like when we married, but I didn't think she'd hold a grudge because I took her away from Carolina barbecue, which I describe as chopped skin with vinegar. But in case she had, I introduced her to Texas barbecue ribs that I'd have flown in from any number of reliable smokehouses in Austin and Fort Worth.

She probably hadn't bargained on Forest Grove, Tennessee, Bison River, South Dakota, or Shackayooka, Ohio, as places to live. I still thought I'd provided her with a more comfortable life than she might have had.

But I found out one evening how strongly she felt about her golf game. She seriously believed that if she'd had the opportunity to work at it, she could have been another Annika Sorenstam.

She brought it up as we were dining at Emily's Steakhouse. We went there every two weeks so I could have my favorite meal—French onion soup, house salad with Ranch dressing, the ten-ounce prime rib medium with real Yorkshire pudding, corn on the cob, and Emily's special dessert, bread pudding with no evil raisins in it.

That night in the middle of dinner, Glenda said, "Charlie Stall thinks I could make it on the tour."

I'm afraid my look gave me away as I said, "Does he really?"

She said, "Do I detect skepticism?"

I said, "I hope Charlie was talking hypothetically."

She said, "He was serious, as a matter of fact."

Charlie was a pleasant enough guy. But you would never know how intelligent he was because he never talked about anything but golf. My guess was, this had caused the breakup of his two previous marriages.

Glenda said, "Charlie is impressed with my short game most of all. He says my set-up reminds him of Tiger Woods. He says I have the right stick, the right grip, and the right stance. Traditional. He says I have length through the bag to keep up with the youngsters on the tour. And he loves my competitive spirit."

I said, "Does Charlie know how old you are?"

She said, "He knows I'm no teenager, yes."

I said, "You're forty-three, Glenda."

She said, "So what? I'm in great shape."

I said, "No question about that. But age takes a toll on any athlete in any game, and the older you are the sooner it happens. Pro sports is a grind. You *do* know this? Please don't tell me Charlie Stall has you thinking about going to the LPGA's qualifying school."

She said, "We've discussed it, yes."

I said, "Listen to me. I've been around sports my whole life, and I can tell you the public playgrounds are loaded with guys who think they could have been Peyton Manning if they'd only caught the right breaks. Glenda, what people *could have been* in this life is what they *are.*"

She said, "You're so fucking supportive, I can hardly stand it."

Not a lot of conversation on the drive home.

TWENTY TWO

AS DINNER conversations go at those AD meetings, there was one I wouldn't mind forgetting from a year ago when Glenda sharpened her wine-aided wit on the unsuspecting.

We were at the Greenbrier and were invited to dine with another AD and his wife in the big room where you dress up in your finest and sit among the blue-green marble pillars.

The other couple was Bobby Wayne Evans and his wife Mopsy. He was the relatively new AD at Coastal Georgia in Savannah, a rising football force in the Sun Belt Conference.

We arrived at the table early, which meant the evening first involved listening to the Scotty Hanson Trio with Colette on vocals. The trio's music was tuneful and familiar, but Colette chose to render talk songs. I despise talk songs—vocalists should sing, not act. I've been meaning to speak harshly to Broadway about this.

Still, it permitted me to dip into my first potato vodka martini and allowed Glenda to dip into the red wine. She'd already fortified herself with two glasses of red in our hotel room when she was deciding on which frock to wear.

We had never met or spent any time with Bobby Wayne Evans and Mopsy. The AD was only two football seasons into the job.

When they joined us, Mopsy said, "Hi, y'all, I'm Mopsy Evans. This is Bobby Wayne. You must be Glenda—I am so pleasured to meet you, and . . ."

"He must be Pete," Glenda said, nodding at me.

"Why of course he is," Mopsy said. "Hi, Pete."

Bobby Wayne was a muscular guy, and Mopsy was in a death struggle to hold on to her Senior Favorite figure—for the sake of the Junior League of Savannah, I imagined. It was easy to see that Bobby Wayne and Mopsy were pleased with their station in life. They were flying the Coastal Georgia colors. They were dressed in red with touches of black and silver. I hadn't been aware that Coastal Georgia wore the same colors as the University of Georgia Bulldogs.

I was blinded by Bobby Wayne's ring. It featured red and black stones on silver, and was slightly smaller than a hubcap. A bauble he received for the Coastal Georgia Varmints winning the Frisky Biscuit Mobile Bowl over the Toledo Rockets. Mopsy wore a red-black-and-silver pendant on a silver chain around her neck. Her bauble for the Varmints beating the Akron Zips in the Dugan's Killer Bug Spray Jacksonville Bowl.

They were kind enough to remove the baubles and give us a grand tour of the ring and pendant.

I receive bowl rings, but I don't wear them like our football coaches do. They use them as recruiting tools. But in that moment I wished I'd brought along my orange-and-gold ring from our victory three years ago over Wake Forest in the Rocco's Pasta Fagioli and Ossobuco Bowl in Orlando.

Glenda held up her glass, and said, "Anybody want to pass the red wine? I'll take anyone at all."

I said, "Are you sure?"

She said, "No, I made that up."

Mopsy said, "Oh, that is *funny*, Glenda."

Glenda said, "It is?"

I refilled Glenda's glass.

Mopsy said cheerfully, "Where are you from originally, Glenda?"

Glenda said, "A place in North Carolina you've never heard of. Flat Beach."

"Carolina? Wonderful!" Mopsy said. "I'm from Carolina. I was born in Highlands. You must know the area, Highlands and Cashiers. It's so lovely."

Glenda said, "I know people go to Highlands to die. I never knew anybody was born there."

Mopsy looked as if she didn't know whether to laugh or not. Then she laughed, and said, "You are hilarious, Glenda. Bobby Wayne, I can't wait to tell Loraine and Ed what she said. They will howl."

Glenda said, "Not too long, I hope . . . Bobby Jones saves Highlands for me."

Mopsy said, "Who?"

Glenda said, "The golfer. As a kid, he spent summers in Highlands."

Mopsy said, "How would you know that, Glenda?"

Glenda said, "I read. Ever tried it?"

Mopsy uttered an "oh" and put her hand over her mouth.

A fellow AD named Spike Roper stopped by the table to say hello. He wore a purple blazer, white slacks, white shirt, a lavender tie with "TCU" spelled out on it in white letters, and purple Nike sneakers. I introduced him to Bobby Wayne and Mopsy. Bobby Wayne seemed excited to meet him. Mopsy couldn't help staring at his shoes.

Glenda said to Spike Roper, "Remind me again what TCU's colors are. I can never remember."

He grinned and moved on.

Bobby Wayne turned to Glenda, and said, "You're from Flat Beach, huh? It sounds like it's on the water."

Glenda said, "It is. The Atlantic Ocean, they call it."

Bobby Wayne said, "I think I know where that is."

Glenda said, "Flat Beach or the Atlantic Ocean?"

Bobby Wayne looked as if he was trying to decide.

Mopsy stared coldly at Bobby Wayne, and said, "You know what? I'm really not hungry. I feel one of my headaches coming on. I hate to duck out on new friends, but . . ."

Glenda said, "I'm sorry, Mopsy. I'm having the brook trout, but I was going to suggest the spaghetti marinara for you. The color would go with your dress."

Mopsy whirled and walked away.

Bobby Wayne said, "Now this is my check. It's on my room. Y'all eat and drink till your belts are tight. Pete, I guess I'll see you at the breakfast meeting."

He dashed off to corral Mopsy and prevent her from grabbing a knife off a dinner table and stabbing somebody.

After a moment, I stood up and said, "Well, Glenda. Care to dance?"

One of the rare occasions when I made *her* laugh.

TWENTY THREE

EDDIE RALPH Stoddard, lawyer to rich people only, called again sometime after lunch to let me know that Dr. Richardson, Dr. Azad, and Dr. Huu had been granted life tenure and substantial raises.

The board's vote was unanimous, not that it had anything to do with whether the professors deserved the rewards. The trustees voted in self-defense. They wanted to avoid a demonstration like the one that disrupted the campus last May. There was evidence that another one might be in the works. A rowdy student group was seen chanting and waving signs that said, "Is Belgium Necessary?" No one was sure of their intentions, but better not to stir them up any more than they were.

My retirement was still on the agenda, but next up was a plan to sell naming rights to buildings, sports facilities, and other objects on the campus. Roy Clapper was convinced that any staunch alumnus would be eager to pay $50,000 a year to have his name on the door to the chancellor's office.

Eddie Ralph said it would read something like, "This Door to the Office of the Chancellor is Presented by Kevin Harold Cunningham, Kappa Sig Pledge Master, '95, B.A., '97."

That kind of thing.

TWENTY FOUR

ASIDE FROM the looting, shooting, and window-breaking, most protests don't amount to more than silly speeches. That was the case with the protest last spring, which got itself started because of—I'm not kidding—butternut. Yes, butternut. The color.

For the historically challenged, butternut was the color of the uniforms worn by the Confederate soldiers in the Civil War. Confederate officers wore gray, as so many movies have reminded us.

What did this have to do with Western Ohio University, a school located in a state that supplied more recruits for the Union army than any other? Or a state that gave birth to four of the Union's most famous generals—Ulysses S. Grant, William Tecumseh Sherman, Philip H. Sheridan, and George Armstrong Custer?

It would not have anything to do with Western Ohio University if it hadn't been for a squirrelly young history professor on our faculty who taught a course called Cleansing the Past. His name was Trotter Chase.

There was no doubt in my mind that Professor Chase, by drumming up the protest, was aiming to see his name added to the list of America's foremost shit-disturbers. Most educated people have other goals.

Trotter Chase aroused the students in his classes to a fever pitch by telling them how he was instantly offended—and so should they be—every time he gazed at the color tan on the uniforms of our football players who participate in what he looked upon as a "prehistoric exercise."

Tan made Trotter see butternut. And butternut did not remind him of our mascot, the cheetah. No. It reminded him of the Confederate uniforms in "that regrettable war."

He had said in the school paper, "The Civil War would not have been waged in the first place if the backward young men of the South hadn't armed themselves and wanted to jump their horses over hedges and shoot at things."

Although the North and South had gone at it more than a hundred and fifty years ago, I didn't think I was alone in finding it troublesome that our high schools and colleges today were turning out students who thought the Civil War was fought over legalizing marijuana, and this was only a short time after the United States had won its independence from China.

When word circulated that a student protest was being organized by a Professor Trotter Chase, a man I'd never laid eyes on, I made the effort to meet him in his office. I learned everything I cared to know about him in that meeting.

One: His long, straight brown hair was parted in the middle and he was wearing tinted glasses. He looked like a young Gloria what's-her-name. If I could have put a poncho on him and draped a string of beads around his neck, I could have thrown him back into the sixties and been done with him. But his look didn't bother me too much. We had football and basketball players who wore tinted glasses and long hair to go with their earrings and necklaces.

Two: I expected him to be wearing a bulky black leather jacket and dark shades. The suicide bomber look. But I was wrong. He was in one of those skimpy little blazers that fits like a sweater and appears to cut off breathing when it's buttoned. Worst men's fashion trend since the Nehru jacket.

Three: He went to Brown. I could deal with that, too, barely. It fascinated me, if I'd heard it right, that students at Brown are permitted to design their own four-year curriculum. I wanted to ask Trotter what he'd majored in at Brown, the movies of Doris Day?

Four: He liked tofu. Coconut curry tofu, preferably. That was a tough one. I will never know what tofu tastes like. To begin with, it sounds like a Japanese comedian.

Five: He was a devoted environmentalist, seriously concerned about the terrors of global warming, climate change, or whatever it's called this moment. Even tougher. He asked if I was troubled about the oceans rising one and a half inches over the next one thousand years? Not really, I said. People would just have to wear shoes with thicker soles.

With the chit-chat out of the way, I stepped into the fray.

I said, "Professor, I could have sworn that a while back every Confederate Battle Flag in the United States had been confiscated, burned, shredded, or sentenced to life in a museum. What do you hope to accomplish with this nonsense you're organizing? What about corn flakes? Do they get off scot free? They're the same color as butternut. I have an old tan sweater at home. It's the color of butternut. I could bring that in and let you stomp on it."

Giving me a look of pity, he said, "There is no deadline to righting the wrongs of history."

I said, "What wrongs are you talking about? The North won the war. Slavery was done away with. The Union was preserved. All good things. And the Union was wise enough to include the Confederate states, apparently aware that the South was going to build some luxurious resorts in the future."

My attempt at levity landed with a thud.

Trotter said, "The fact is, the hideous Confederate flag can still be seen in pockets of the South and even the Midwest . . . and we have yet to demolish the statues and monuments honoring the traitors."

I said, "Young man, you're bringing out the cheese grits in me. You're referring to the Confederate *Battle* Flag, not the flag of the Confederacy. The Battle Flag was designed so it wouldn't be confused with the Stars and Stripes on the battlefield. Some people see that flag as a symbol of bravery, not slavery."

He said, "I find it more repulsive than the swastika."

I laughed and said, "That's a hard reach, son. But you have to agree with one thing about the swastika—it was a hell of a logo."

No laugh. I said, "As for the traitors, I take it you mean traitors like Robert E. Lee, Stonewall Jackson, Jeb Stuart, and those other Southerners who graduated from the United States Military Academy at West Point. Nearly every high-ranking Confederate officer fought for the United States in the Mexican-American and Seminole wars earlier in their careers. To me, that service counts for something."

Trotter said, "Yes, well, to me, it means they must have missed the course on good judgment while they were at West Point."

I said, "There are ten army posts that are still named for Confederate generals today, and they're honored for their gallantry as *soldiers*, not rebels."

"I wasn't aware there are ten, but I'm sure you can name them," he said.

I said, "You bet your ass I can. Fort Lee, Fort Hood, Fort Bragg, Fort A. P. Hill . . . and Benning, Pickett, Polk, Gordon, Rucker, and Camp Beauregard. Let me lay some facts on you about those men."

"I'd rather you didn't bother," he said.

I said, "I insist. It happens that General Robert E. Lee freed his slaves in 1862, a year *before* the Emancipation Proclamation, and three years before the South surrendered."

"That sure lets him off the hook with me," Trotter smirked.

I said, "General John Bell Hood, a U.S. cavalry officer, was wounded fighting the Comanche in Texas before the Civil War. He fought in almost every major battle. Lost a leg at Gettysburg and an arm at Chickamauga.

"General A. P. Hill served in the U.S. Army for fifteen years before joining the Confederacy. He was one of the South's fiercest commanders, a hero at Antietam, and he was killed in action at Petersburg.

"General Henry Benning had three horses shot out from under him in battles, and led a successful assault at Gettysburg.

"General George Pickett was a wealthy man who served in the U.S. Army and fought in the Mexican-American War, like most of the others. He was an outspoken opponent of slavery and switched to the Confederate cause to defend his homeland. Of course he'll always be known for 'Pickett's Charge' at Gettysburg."

"Speaking of stupidity," the professor said.

I said, "He was a military man—he followed orders. I'm always moved by what he said to his troops before the charge on Cemetery Ridge. Don't go teary-eyed on me while I repeat it. 'Up, men, and to your posts. For your wives, your mothers, your sweethearts, your homes, and the glory of Old Virginia!'"

"More Southern stupidity," the professor said.

"General Braxton Bragg," I went on, "was another U.S. Army hero in the Mexican-American War and Seminole Wars. He led his troops to a win in the Battle of Chickamauga, one of the South's major victories.

"General John Brown Gordon was wounded at Antietam, the Wilderness, and Chickamauga. After the war he became a United States senator from Georgia.

"General Leonidas Polk was killed in the Battle of Atlanta . . . and Edmund Rucker, who was in truth a colonel, not a general, lost an arm in the Battle of Nashville."

"They deserved it," the professor said.

Ignoring that, I said, "I wouldn't want to overlook General P. G. T. Beauregard. Only in Louisiana could anyone be named Pierre Gustave Toutant Beauregard. He served in the U.S. Army for twenty-three years before joining the Confederacy. He's the guy who ordered the shelling on Fort Sumter, and he later fought at First Manassas and Shiloh."

"Thank you," Trotter said. "This has been most informative."

I said, "Incidentally, after you finish knocking down the Confederate statues and monuments, you can start scraping Abe Lincoln's face off Mount Rushmore. Yeah, he freed the slaves, but he wanted to ship the black folks off to the Bahamas or somewhere. And while you're at it, righting these wrongs, you may want to knock down the Washington Monument. It's rumored old George, the father of our country, was a slave-owner himself."

Trotter said, "Do we have anything else to discuss? I have a class."

I said, "Just one more thing. You say you're an environmentalist, right?"

He said, "I am a *militant* environmentalist."

I said, "I'm okay with that, even though I'm a man who wants his car to start, his TV to work, his lights to come on, and prefers living in a house that stays cool in the summer and warm in the winter."

He said, "I rather imagined you would say something like that."

I said, "I just want to make myself clear. I do understand the need for environmentalists."

He said, "I'm pleased to hear it."

I said, "Seriously, I do. But I think that if you're really dedicated to the cause, you should have to live naked in a forest."

His mouth dropped open. If I'd had a football with me, I'd have spiked it on the way out of his office.

TWENTY FIVE

SPRING is always the best time for protests. You rarely see activists crawl out of a snowbank or come sliding across the ice to scream and holler that everything you like to eat will soon be banned, and it will be against the law for anyone to own guns in this country except street gangs and criminals.

Professor Chase checked the long-range weather forecast and picked a pleasant spring day for his protest. With the aid of the Internet, he hit a payload of sillies that showed up. Most of them came to demonstrate on behalf of their own causes while others were hired at $15 an hour by protest reps to yell about political issues of one kind or another.

Rita Jo and I had made our own plans to level the playing field. We were privately given the approval of Chancellor Warren Carpenter and Roy Clapper to do this, although they retained deniability.

"This is great," I said as Rita Jo and I were tossing ideas back and forth. "It's going to be spring break for the demonstrators minus the outdoor screwing on Florida beaches."

She said, "Heck, let's don't take away *all* the fun."

We recruited helpers from among the athletes, cheerleaders, Cheetah Girls, the band, the Greeks, the Performing Arts department, and the Dub Spurlock College of Communications.

The students made their own signs and costumes. Some impersonated the homeless, which required large cardboard boxes to sit in. Others went for the welfare look. Guys blended Ralph Lauren with Under Armour. Young women wore what they call yoga pants with tank tops. Both groups wandered around looking for the kiosk where they could score food stamps.

Rita Jo organized our marching band. She split it into two groups. Half of them wore Union blue, the other half wore Confederate gray—or butternut if they could find any.

She arranged things so that when the appropriate time came, which was when Professor Trotter Chase took the mic on the steps of Old Ad, the two groups of band members quick-stepped from behind the building, one group playing and singing "The Battle Hymn of the Republic" and the other group playing and singing "Dixie."

It was perfect timing. Professor Chase had just thumped on the mic and said, "My concerned Americans . . ." Then the music drowned him out.

Rita Jo said her favorite verse from the Battle Hymn was, "As he died to make men holy, let us live to make men free. Glory, glory, hallelujah."

I said, "That *is* inspiring, but so is my favorite verse from the other team's fight song."

She said, "Which is . . . ?"

I said, "'There's buckwheat cakes and Injun batter, makes you fat or a little fatter. Look away, Dixie Land.'"

She punched me on the arm and led me into the world of signs, protesters, turquoise belt buckles, Navajo beads, jars of pills for sale, and food wagons. We stopped to have beef tacos at Maximilian and Carlota's Taco Wacko. The illegal immigration sauce was fabulous.

There were incoherent speeches going on everywhere by wild-eyed men and women. Some were snarling, some were slobbering. Some were defending wars, others were boycotting wars. A woman who looked like she hadn't bathed or washed her hair in a year was holding a sign that said, "Free Speech Can Be Emotionally Disturbing."

A TV cameraman took a shot of her, but soon ducked away from the odor.

We came upon a well-fed young girl in cut-off jeans standing in the shade with a sign that said, "I Want My Fresh Air Back."

I said to her, "Who took your fresh air, if I may ask?"

She said, "Big business . . . wasn't it?"

I said, "I wonder what big business did with it? Any idea?"

She said, "The guy told me they sell it and become bigger businesses. He says it ought to be against the law to do that."

I said, "What guy told you this?"

She said, "Look, man. I don't want to get anybody in trouble. I only know this guy gave me fifteen dollars to stand here and hold this sign for two hours."

Next we were drawn to the sign that said "Open Borders Now!" and to the young couple that sat cross-legged on the grass under the sign.

Rita Jo said, "Want to go chat with Donny and Marie?"

We walked over to the couple.

"I have a question," I said to the guy.

He said, "It's not about math, is it?"

I said, "Aren't you people aware that we already have open borders?"

The girl said, "But they aren't open enough, are they? Like, have you seen anybody going to Kansas lately? Nebraska?"

I said, "Now that you mention it . . ."

The girl said, "It's the only way to stop terrorism for sure. It's a desert thing, isn't it? Deserts are really big. Terrorists grow up with nothing to eat but sand. There's no water to drink *anywhere*. Not everybody can live next door to the *Nile*, can they? It's like, where's the snack bar, man? This is why the terrorists are angry. I mean, *really* angry. Don't you get it?"

Rita Jo bit her lip.

The girl said, "So, what we do is, we let them come here and introduce them to Krispy Kreme donuts, Jack in the Box chicken sandwiches, Whataburgers, and bottled water. Other good stuff. They find out what a great place America is. They relax and watch cable and don't have to cut off everybody's heads anymore. It's pretty simple, if you stop to think about it."

Rita Jo looked at me. "Smarter now?"

We turned away.

■ ▣ ▣

FROM THERE, we moved over to the tall, muscular Confederate general in a gray tunic, gold sash, and black cavalry hat with a plume. He wore a fake beard and was sipping from a plastic cup filled with what I gathered was an alcoholic beverage, and held a sign that said, "I Wish I Was in Dixie—or Her Sister."

I thought I knew him.

"Just back from Shiloh, are we?" I said. "You don't look scathed."

He said, "How you doing, Mr. Wallace."

It was Riley "Farm Dog" Holt, our two-year All-America linebacker. He would be graduating in a week with a degree in geology, I'm proud to say. Earlier in the spring he'd been drafted in the first round by the Green Bay Packers.

I said to Rita Jo, "You did this?"

"He volunteered," she said.

I said to Riley, "You catching any heat?"

"Naw," he said. "Most people laugh and go fetch me another cocktail. Your professor stopped by. He frowned at my uniform. Said I should be ashamed of myself. I told him to toddle on off or he'd be late for his blowjob."

I stared at the ground, shook my head.

Riley said, "He said he was going to report me to the dean of student affairs for using indecent language to a superior. I told him I'm outta here next week, I'm just waitin' on a train. I asked him who the dean of student affairs was. I didn't know we had one. He said she was Dr. Fatima Bahar. I said, 'Sounds like an A-rab. All robe, no tits.'"

Rita Jo said, "You didn't say that?"

Riley shrugged with a grin.

I knew Dr. Bahar. She spent most of her time hacking into the Facebooks and emails of students to see if any of them were practicing—or defending—free speech so she could suspend them for an indefinite period. The chancellor spent a good bit of his own time lifting her suspensions.

▣ ▣ ▣

SOMETHING caught Rita Jo's eye.

She said, "You have to come hear this guy. I recruited him from the parking lot at the West Side Mall."

She dragged me over to a man in a beard, ponytail, headband, grimy safari jacket, baggy jeans, and army boots. He stood on an upside-down wash tub. Rita Jo borrowed my iPhone, told it to do something, and we listened to the guy for as long as I could. This much was preserved:

". . . and if we were here on this Earth today, alive and breathing, which we are not, you would feel the same as you do right now. Like a human. But we're not here. We're in the first stage of the Big Journey. I can tell you the exact date and time that God willed the world to be vaporized. It was at 4:37 in the afternoon—drive time—on February 13, 1979. The day rap went mainstream.

"I was standing on the corner of 42nd Street and Seventh Avenue in New York City with my axe. I'd been out of work for twenty-two years—ever since Elvis invented the guitar. The sound of the vaporization was like a big whoosh. It was like, you know, this weird wind came out of nowhere and sucked us up. The whole world and all the people in it were gone for five minutes. White people, black people, tan people, polka-dot people. I'd seen those polka-dot people somewhere before, but I can't remember where.

"Anyway, there was this lull, and I saw things, man. Lot of dead people. I saw a guy dressed like Shakespeare, but it could have been Errol Flynn. I saw Satchmo. He was riffing on 'Pretty Girl Stomp.' Then all of a sudden we were hit by another whoosh. That's when I saw God.

"He was standing there, smiling at me. I know you're curious. What does God look like? The big question. I can tell you now, man. He looks like Gregory Peck. And the chick with him . . ."

Rita Jo said, "Would you have guessed Gregory Peck?"

I said, "I'm sure a couple of ministers I know will be fascinated with the news."

■ ■ ■

WE CONTINUED to wander when we spotted my wife.

Glenda was strolling with Charlie Stall. My wife was in a golf outfit, wearing a short navy blue skirt with a red and white knit shirt, a white visor, and white golf shoes. The short skirt showed off her tan legs.

Rita Jo said, "I haven't seen the missus in a while. My gracious, she's the color of butternut."

I laughed at that. Couldn't help it.

When we caught up with them, Glenda and Rita Jo touched cheeks daintily with fake smiles.

Charlie flashed a big grin and gave me a crushing handshake.

I said to the pro, "Shouldn't you be curing somebody's slice today?"

"It's slow at the Oak," he said. "Everybody's over here, checking out the protest action."

"What do you think?" I asked Glenda.

She said, "It looks festive. This is what you and Rita arranged to undermine the professor?"

"We gave it our best shot," Rita Jo said.

I said to Glenda, "This is more people than we expected today. Where did you find a place to park?"

Glenda said, "At the Town Club. I took Charlie to lunch. We walked over from there."

Rita Jo said, "I love that old club. The food's great."

Glenda said, "I didn't know you were a member, Rita."

Rita Jo smiled, and said, "Oh, I'm not . . . but your husband is."

Glenda gave me a look that would have stopped Ohio State on Michigan's goal line.

Charlie Stall said, "It looks like you have something here for everybody. I see everything but a driving net."

Rita Jo said, "I thought of that, but I didn't want to include Glenda's sport among the morons."

Glenda said, "That was sweet of you, Rita. We'll leave it to you and my husband to enjoy the fun you've organized. There's the margarita stand, Charlie. Let's give it a try."

They walked away, arm-in-arm.

We stared at them.

Rita Jo said, "I think I pissed Glenda off. Sorry."

I said, "Don't worry about it. All in all, my wife does an okay job of handling our relationship."

Rita Jo said, "*Our* relationship? You and me? Us?"

I said, "Yeah. You know . . . like most wives, I'm sure Glenda would be happier if my deputy looked more like Frau Blücher than Rita Jo Foster."

She said, "What am I supposed to do about that?"

"Nothing," I said. "As I recall, looking good *is* part of your job description."

She playfully elbowed me, and we continued strolling.

TWENTY SIX

A COUPLE of minutes later we saw the sign that said, "Vote No on Buttercup"—Rita Jo's doing—and we noticed Trotter Chase move into the crowd around the young man who stood by the sign. We joined in.

Trotter said to the young man, "Your sign is wrong."

The young man said, "What sign?"

The professor said, "The one you are holding up. It should say butterNUT, not butterCUP. Someone has played a trick."

The guy said, "You fucking with me, man?"

Trotter said, "No, I'm trying to be helpful."

The guy said, "Man, all I'm holding is Storm Cloud Haze. Super shit. Straight out of Denver. Here, have a hit."

He handed the joint to Trotter. Trotter took a hit and evidently found it to be more powerful than anything he'd experienced. The hit changed his life forever. Three weeks after the protest, he resigned from the university and from teaching altogether and moved to San Francisco with Rolf, his roommate.

I couldn't blame Trotter for choosing San Francisco. It's a beautiful city. I like going there, although I have two problems with it. One, the residents. Those who look at me with great sorrow because I'm not as smart as they are to live there. Two, the food. It's the only city in the United States where you can't get a hotdog without foam on it.

A year ago Rita Jo and I were there for an NCAA convention and I made the mistake of playing big shot and inviting two other athletic directors and their wives to join us for dinner at a hot new restaurant a local acquaintance had told me not to miss.

I still don't know the name of it. The sign was a mixture of letters, some upside down, some backward. You had to have the address to find the place.

The first course was a long platter of something that looked like lime-green cotton candy. You were supposed to grab handfuls of it and put it in your mouth before it evaporated.

The second course looked like a display of candied insects.

The third course was a squirt of pink shampoo curling around a black leaf.

Finally, the entrée. A tiny orange sponge that quivered on the plate.

I never knew what any of it tasted like. I dined on the reliable green olives in my three martinis.

The check was only $10,456.

■ ■ ■

IT WAS months later when we heard news of Trotter Chase from someone on our faculty who'd kept up with him. The word circulated with warp speed. Trotter and Rolf, after moving to San Francisco, took their time deciding where to live, the city offering so many quaint neighborhoods. Only Oakland was out of bounds, but they planned to go see what Oakland was all about someday, once they'd found a way to obtain handguns.

They settled on a spacious apartment on one of San Francisco's hills that offered a view of *everything,* as Trotter related to friends back here.

It turned out that Rolf, the roommate, had inherited a fortune from his dead father in Gothenburg, Sweden. His father had built an enormously successful machinery company. Rolf never knew what the company did, other than manufacture little things that made big things work. Rolf sold the company and was disappointed to learn that the fortune wasn't enough to buy the San Francisco 49ers, which he thought would have been a fun thing to do.

Seeking a new career, Trotter enrolled in one of San Francisco's colleges of culinary arts. Rolf bankrolled him in a business venture. He bought an Italian restaurant in the trendy Embarcadero that had failed because the owner refused to speak English to the customers. Rolf spent a ton remodeling the space and they turned it into another trendy restaurant where Trotter was performing as the head chef.

The name of the joint is *Le Cochon et Le Chou-fleur*. That's French for pig and cauliflower, Rita Jo informed me, whether I wanted to know it or not. I slipped that piece of information in there with "*Où est Passé Roger?*"

Perfect, is what I thought about Trotter's new career.

Let him join the comedy scene of fine dining in San Francisco instead of poisoning the minds of naïve college students.

TWENTY SEVEN

ABOUT A WEEK after the protest gala, Glenda fixed dinner for us at home. It was something she did on the average of twice a year. We dined out a lot. Dinner was her old reliable—steak, baked potato, green salad. Unfortunately, I spoiled the evening by bringing up Charlie Stall.

I said, "By the way, Glenda, if you and Charlie are going to stroll around arm-in-arm in public, I'd appreciate it if you didn't do it in front of our friends, athletes, and faculty. They might get the wrong impression."

"Like what kind of wrong impression?" she said.

I said, "Like some of them might think there's something going on between the two of you."

She said, "Charlie is a good friend and my golf teacher. I can't help it if there are small-minded people who want to believe there's anything else to it."

I said, "I'm just saying there are people who always want to think the worst of people, and in my job I'd prefer not to be one of their targets."

She said, "What Charlie and I have in common is a love of golf, and if certain people can't handle that, it's their problem."

I said, "I'm more than aware of Charlie's love for golf. Do me a favor. Send up a flare if he ever has a conversation on another subject."

She said, "Since you've brought up relationships, I wonder what some people think about you and your little girlfriend? You and Rita give new meaning to the word inseparable. You two stroll around looking like you're joined at the hip—or in some other location."

I let that pass, and said, "You damn well know how close we work together."

"So do Charlie and I," she said.

I said, "But Rita Jo and I work for Western Ohio University. She's my *deputy*, or has that slipped your mind?"

She said, "Thanks for reminding me. I'll stop thinking of her playing cupcake to your Mister Darcy."

I said, "I can't keep those British movies straight. Is that the one where everybody wears three layers of clothing and lives in a castle?"

"Very funny," she said. "*The Tonight Show* called. They want you on."

"I'm busy arguing," I said.

She said, "You know what? The first three or four years Rita was on your staff, I thought she'd be married and gone any minute. With her looks, how could she not be?"

I said, "I thought the same thing."

Glenda said, "So why is she still here?"

I said, "She loves her job. And she keeps saying she hasn't met the right man yet. She goes out with guys all the time, as you well know."

"But not for long," Glenda said. "When we dine with Rita and her dates, the men all look suitable to me. Nice-looking, well-to-do. But none of them last. Two dates, three, and they're done. Stick a fork in them."

"I chalk it up to another one of life's mysteries," I said.

"But it isn't," she said. "Pete, you're not blind and you're not a moron. You are her idol, if not something more than that, which I don't care to get into this evening."

I said, "Glenda, how many times do I have to say this? I've never laid a glove on Rita Jo, and she's never laid a glove on me. And if we *had*, you would know it. Smart women pick up on things like that. I've read that in a book. There are plenty of married guys who obviously aren't aware of this fact. They're the true morons. Which I guess explains the high divorce rate in this country."

She said, "Boy, did I strike a nerve."

I said, "You did, but not the kind you think. Yes, Rita Jo is flat-out good-looking. No sane person would argue with that. Yes, she's absolutely invaluable to me in my job . . . and to the university, in fact. And yes, we've grown extremely close through the years. But if there's any love involved, it's the kind you find between devoted friends."

"Oh, please," she said with a look.

I said, "I can't be more honest than that, Glenda."

She said, "Well, at least you've spared me one thing."

I said, "What?"

She said, "Thank God you didn't say she's the sister you never had."

TWENTY EIGHT

IN MY continuing effort to take you behind the scenes in the life of a dutiful athletic director, a glance at a photo on my office wall reminds me that I haven't really touched on basketball.

It's a photo of Adidas Nike Smith. He's hovering above the rim with a wide grin about to complete one of his rotorhead, disposal, whoa-daddy dunks for which he'd gained fame and adulation.

In the two seasons we had him, Adidas Nike Smith became the greatest hoopster to wear the orange and tan. It's a shame that later in his life he became the greatest embarrassment that ever wore the orange and tan.

Adidas Nike is his real name, incidentally. I laughed when I found that out. But I'm more likely to laugh at names with hyphens in them. I couldn't avoid a chuckle the time I was introduced to a famous English cricket player named Christopher Derek Fox-Pippert.

Adidas Nike could out-leap a kangaroo and hang in the air like Cirque du Soleil. He was our first basketball All-American. Made first-team AP both seasons before he left us to go pro seven years ago.

He stood six nine and poured in 35 to 40 points a game. He could pop a 3 without looking at the rim. It seemed like the bucket went racing around the arena looking for his shot. He brought so much talent to the hardwood, he made "Kindly Doc" Shaffer almost look like a coach. We didn't win a conference title or reach the playoffs with Adidas Nike, but he put fans in the seats.

We were still taking pride in him until two winters ago when for no reason other than to draw attention to himself, Adidas Nike shot his mouth off to a writer for a European sports magazine about the lack of an education he received when he was in college.

In that one interview Adidas Nike caused me more trouble than the butternut professor, who was a dish of peach cobbler by comparison.

"Kindly Doc" Shaffer had recruited Adidas Nike out of Willard Harvin High School in South Chicago, a neighborhood where a St. Valentine's Day Massacre occurs every weekend among the hoodrats and all-out gangs while the city's cops and politicians refuse to show any interest in it.

In Adidas Nike's application I noticed that after twelve years of elementary school, junior high, and high school, he could spell his name correctly, but that was about it. He spelled his hometown "Chicargo," spelled his high school "Woolin Hacker," and "boopsker" was how he spelled his favorite sport of basketball.

But it wasn't completely his fault.

His application and others I'd seen told me everything I cared to know about the pathetic state of our public school system, and what a swell organization the American Federation of Teachers has become.

It appears to me that the only words today's public school students learn from their teachers are "sabbatical," "substitute," "strike," "called in sick," and the old reliable "car won't start." And you can't fire them.

I took a chance on Adidas Nike, and I'd do it again, like any other AD or coach would have. We considered it a miracle that we won out on him over Kentucky, Louisville, and UConn.

Rita Jo found him a tutor and someone to drag him to as many classes as possible. I was concentrating on football and didn't question it when "Kindly Doc" Shaffer said he would sign him up for American History and other courses that might help him appreciate this great nation.

Then I found out what he was studying. A heavy-duty lineup of Human Activity, People Resources, Sports Discussion, and African-American Studies.

I'm ashamed to say I didn't do anything about it. Instead, I contributed to the problem. I signed off on giving Adidas Nike an apartment with maid service in a complex near the campus, a charge card to Emily's Steakhouse, the loan of a Lexus, and a cost-of-living allowance of $1,200 a month under the most recent NCAA guidelines.

My thanks for that was him spouting off to a publication called *Gigantes Del Basket*, a basketball magazine in Europe, published in Madrid, about how he was never taught anything in college.

He was quoted saying, "I was there to make residue for the college. I took paper classes, which I didn't have to attend. Somebody wrote papers for me so I could stay legible."

Naturally the AP picked it up, so did Reuters, and so did our own hometown *Clarion Tribune*, which slapped us around with what I considered to be a little too much pleasure.

The *Clarion Tribune*'s young sports editor Teddy Aycock did this despite the dozens of lunches and dinners I'd bought him at the Town Club, and after all the home-game football tickets I'd given him to sell for profit, and the cut-rate price Rita Jo had obtained for him to buy a Honda Civic.

Pain-in-the-ass media.

Like the saying goes, you can't live with 'em and you can't kill 'em.

■ ■ ■

ADIDAS NIKE didn't drop out of school because we hadn't taught him anything. He dropped out to collect the $12 million the New York Knicks paid him. But he failed to be what the Knicks thought he'd be.

We heard he'd become a troublemaker. He missed meetings. He didn't like passing the ball to his teammates. The Knicks cut him after two seasons for being a "disruptive influence." No other NBA team wanted to take a chance on him, so he went to play in the Euroleague.

He was with five different clubs in six years. He started off with the Berlin Albatrosse, was traded to the Milan Red Shoes, traded to the Moscow Horses, traded to the Belgrade Stars, and finally found his niche as the starting small forward for the Real Madrid Los Blancos, or The Whites. Even I could translate that.

I could guess that Adidas Nike popped off because he wanted his one-time fans back here to know he was alive and had found success and was enjoying bowls of *paella* no matter how many living things were swimming in it.

He said the school put him in African-American Studies, thinking they were doing him a favor, but it hadn't been a favor at all.

He said in the article, "I've never considered myself an African-American. I'm a black man born in the United States and I'm as American as any white man born in the United States. I've never been to Africa and I ain't going. Why would anybody go unless they like runnin' from lions and leopards and shit?"

I agreed with him on that, having been born a Texan-American. I wish I'd discussed it with him when he was with us. Naturally there were members of the faculty who were so outraged over what they called the "scandal" they could barely digest their egg-white omelets.

The loudest squeals came from Dr. Edith Lawson. She said to the *Clarion Tribune*, "This is exactly what I have been complaining about. Our athletic department is guilty of academic fraud. I know for a fact that these 'paper classes' exist, and someday I intend to prove it."

Dr. Keith Kurth followed up with, "The athletic department has plunged this university into a cave of evils. As an educator, I am particularly saddened by these revelations."

Dr. Karl "Red Alert" Davis, a bearded shrimp with a gimpy leg who taught communism in the Political Science department, took it upon himself to call the *Columbus Dispatch*, the *Cleveland Plain Dealer*, and the *Cincinnati Enquirer*, and give each paper the same heartfelt opinion on the matter.

His statement was, "If I am to believe Adidas Nike Smith, I am forced to say the adults have failed the children. I do wish that weren't his real name."

Our damage control committee consisted of me, Rita Jo, Roy Clapper, Coach Taggert, Coach Dixon, and Chancellor Carpenter.

The chancellor opened the meeting with, "Okay, folks. How are we going to shut up our academic people and dig our way out of this cesspool?"

I said, "All I know to do is give everybody on the faculty life tenure and their own seventy-five-inch flatscreen hi-def Sony."

"Pete, this is no time for humor," the chancellor said.

Rita Jo said, "We need a statement from Coach Shaffer. He's living full-time in his fishing cabin in Wisconsin. I have his cell number. He'll pick up if I can catch him when he's not wrestling with a walleye."

Rita Jo said we definitely needed statements from me, the chancellor, and as many of Adidas Nike's Big U. teammates as we could track down.

Flip Dixon said, "I have my statement ready if a reporter calls. It wasn't me, I wasn't here, and I don't understand the question."

Coach Tag said, "If this shit spills over onto my football program, I'll personally fly to Spain and do to Adidas Nike what Bill Russell would have done to Michael Jordan."

I said, "What was that?"

The coach said, "Grab him in mid-air, tie his arm in a knot, and say, 'Now shoot, big man.'"

Chancellor Carpenter's statement read: "It is disappointing any time a former student is unhappy with his or her experience at our university. I welcome the opportunity to talk to this student-athlete about returning here to continue his studies, as I have welcomed back other student-athletes interested in completing their degrees."

The best Rita Jo could pry out of "Kindly Doc" Shaffer was: "I don't recognize anything he's talking about. Paper classes? Don't they require paper in most classes, except if there's a computer? It's not fair for him to portray me or the school as doing anything other than trying to win games."

You had to say he was truthful.

Rita Jo said my words for public consumption bordered on brilliant, mainly because she helped me write them.

I, or we, said:

I have been in touch with many of Adidas Nike Smith's teammates, and I have found them to be adamant that they had a different academic experience at Western Ohio than the one described by him. They have been affected deeply by his remarks. In line with that, I have hired a distinguished lawyer in this state, a former Federal prosecutor, Mr. Dylan Alderman, a graduate of this university, to conduct an independent investigation into any and all past academic and athletic irregularities, if indeed they exist. I have the utmost confidence that Mr. Alderman's thorough investigation will find no evidence of any wrong-doing on our part.

It didn't, as we know.

The scandal slowly disappeared, and Chancellor Carpenter threw a victory dinner for the damage control committee at the Town Club.

TWENTY NINE

NOT TOO many years ago you would have had to strap me down on a sled and command a pack of Alaskan huskies to drag me to a women's college basketball game. I'd bought into the hearsay that lady hoopsters couldn't dribble past mid-court without tripping over their own sneakers, could seldom jump high enough to clear a street curb, and shot a peanut at the bucket.

It is a fact that the basketball used in the women's game is one inch smaller in circumference than the ball used by the men. And the 3-point arc in the women's game is one foot shorter than the men's.

Those rules are in place due to the scientific fact that women in general have smaller hands than men. But those two rules make no difference whatever when you look at the athleticism on display today by the college girls.

No sport in history has made as much progress in so short a time as women's hoops. That's something the dumbest sumbitch in the world can't argue with, and I'm able to argue it with the loudest voice in the room because I used to be one of the dumb sumbitches. I was Joe Bob Six-Pack.

Women's hoops didn't exist at the Big U., and it still might not if it hadn't been for Rita Jo. She tried to talk me into starting up the program nine years ago. It took me four years to get around to it. My only excuse was that I was busy trying to move football into high society.

But Rita Jo kept after me, saying I'd be astonished today to see the ponytails and headbands flying up and down the court. She made me watch video highlights of the girls who've lifted the game to heights unknown. I watched clips of Cheryl Miller at USC, Sheryl Swoopes at Texas Tech, Chamique Holdsclaw, Tamika Catchings, and Candace Parker at Tennessee, and Sue Bird, Diana Taurasi, and Maya Moore at UConn. Pat Summitt at Tennessee put lady hoops on the map, and Geno Auriemma built an incredible dynasty at UConn. Rita Jo put it in a way I could understand. She said Pat Summitt and Geno Auriemma were the Bear Bryant and Woody Hayes of women's hoops.

Rita Jo also said, "The women's game is drawing amazing crowds these days, not only at Tennessee and UConn, but at Baylor, OU, Notre Dame, Stanford, Texas. Why not Western Ohio?"

I said, "Keep selling me."

She said, "People in this town need something else to do in the winter besides scrape the ice off their windshields. Some go to our men's games, but they don't go to movies anymore. Nobody goes to movies now but twelve-year-olds who like to scream and cringe when the dinosaurs eat the airplanes."

She continued, "Adults can find any movie they want to see on cable at home, and shove their own popcorn in the microwave. Women's hoops will give our fans another opportunity to leave the house. If we can build a winning program, it'll give us a third revenue sport, and you'll be saying women's basketball is the best thing to come out of Title IX."

She sold me. When I agreed to install the program five years ago, I told Rita Jo she could start by finding us a good coach.

"I already have," she said.

The person she had in mind was Rosemary Donahue at Indiana Tech. The lady had paid her dues as an assistant coach at Stanford, North Carolina, LSU, and Tennessee. She'd finally been given a head coaching job and she'd been putting winning teams on the court ever since.

"What'll she cost me?" I asked.

Rita Jo said, "She'll come for five-fifty, plus perks for winning."

I said, "You've discussed this with her?"

"Twice," she said.

I said, "Rosemary Donahue sounds Catholic."

"Did I hear a siren go off?" Rita Jo said. "She *is* a Catholic, Pete, but you'd have to twist her arm to find it out. She has a swell husband, Steve. He's a successful house-builder. Their two children will be entering high school soon. I've told Rosemary you'll get them into St. Paul Prep."

"That was thoughtful of you," I said.

She said, "If you can't, I can. I know the headmaster."

"Another shock," I said. "And just to have it on record, I'm not frightened of Catholics. Not unless one of them comes at me with a crucifix bigger than a parking meter."

Rita Jo said, "Trust me, Pete. Rosemary won't limit her recruiting to virgins, if that's worrying you. And if she finds out that her best player is gay, I assure you she won't try to force her to enter a reprogramming clinic."

I said, "What does Rosemary look like?"

"Attractive blue-eyed brunette," Rita Jo said. "She's a little taller than me. She has a commanding presence. She's a competitor. You can see it in her eyes. She was an all-conference forward at Stanford. She *knows* the game."

"Go get her," I said.

She said, "I'm on it."

▣ ▣ ▣

THERE'S nothing like a winner to improve an AD's health and attitude about life. Rosemary Donahue began by recruiting intelligence and speed, and she still does. She produced an 18-12 record her first season with a patchwork lineup of freshmen and junior college transfers. To my delight, she'd kept on winning, and her teams have become more skilled, more aggressive, more confident.

As a money-grubbing athletic director, I can say that the best thing about her accomplishments was that her teams have gone from drawing 600 fans the first year to over 3,000 in no time. Women's basketball had yet to pay for itself, but it was getting close.

Rita Jo enjoyed watching my enthusiasm grow for the women's game. I liked to sit behind our bench and listen to what goes on. Rosemary dresses fashionably for games and strolls the courtside with her arms folded and never loses control over an absurd foul call or a player's bumbling mistake. I was impressed by her demeanor, particularly since I'd been a football coach who would lapse into blind rages and speak in an unknown tongue to my players and the zebras.

In a game against Illinois her second season, I watched Rosemary summon a player off the bench and say in a calm voice, "Twenty-Two is killing us from the corner. Get on her. If she's still breathing after two minutes, double her with Teresa and break her damn leg."

From the start, it was predictable that our successful men's coach, Flip Dixon, a macho guy, would try to embarrass Rosemary when they first met in my office.

"What's your ideal offense?" he asked her.

She said, "Twin towers if I have two. But you always need outside shooters, don't you?"

Flip said, "What if you don't have a post player?"

Rosemary said, "I go with a spread. What you call the Donut. All you can do is try to create cuts and penetrations."

Flip said, "How would you attack a zone?"

Rosemary said, "I prefer the one-three-one, but the overload can work. No zone is perfect. There's always a weak spot in it. Find it and pick on it."

Flip said, "What do you do if your shooters are having a cold night?"

Rosemary said, "They can still rebound and play defense. Are you scoring, Pete? How am I doing?"

I grinned. Flip Dixon didn't.

I was forced to referee between the two. Rule on their complaints over raises for their assistants, court time for practices, office space, travel arrangements, seating for friends at home games, and training table food. If Flip wanted more beef and potatoes, Rosemary wanted more veal and pasta.

Court time was a constant problem. We worked out a practice schedule where the men and women would alternate taking the court first. But whichever team it was, that team would stay twenty or thirty minutes longer than they should. Not every time, but too often for a man with other sports to worry about.

I'd heard from other ADs that when you have men and women basketball teams, you're going to have affairs, breakups, emotional dramas. But I never knew it could be as vicious as it was until Coach Dixon recorded a conversation between the two teams as they were passing each other in the corridor leading to the court at practice sessions. He asked for a meeting that involved himself, Rosemary, Rita Jo, and me.

That's where he played the tape in front of us, but primarily in an effort to embarrass Rosemary.

On the tape was a mixture of male and female voices responding to each other. We heard:

"Ho."

"Pig."

"Bitch."

"Piss Pad."

"Free Gash."

"Buttwipe."

"Chomp on this."

"Eat my lap."

"Trim Bim."

"Rotate, baby."

"Here's your dinner."

"You wish."

"Toxic slut."

"Pencil Dick."

I said we'd heard enough. Flip turned off the tape. I asked him what the point was? Flip said he wanted Rosemary to hear the kind of players she's recruiting. He added, "Men talk like that, but women shouldn't."

I looked at Rosemary, and said, "Would you care to respond?"

She said, "I thought my ladies won easily."

THIRTY

IF AND WHEN I do get around to trying to write a book I know I'll have to devote a fair amount of time to the non-revenue sports, which are known to most athletic directors as a plague on the human race.

I give you college baseball, for the first example. In our case, baseball has been about as non-revenue as you can get.

Baseball is a sport I still like despite its consistent effort to bore younger generations to death. Baseball was the national pastime when I was a kid and the world moved slower. That was before the National Football League bought up the sports sections of America's daily newspapers—and the national pastime came with them in a package deal. First thing they did was erase the national pastime from conversation, and then they made the Dallas Cowboys "America's Team."

In my youth it didn't make any difference if I was sitting in a minor league ballpark cheering for the Amarillo Gold Sox, or watching a major league game on TV, it was comforting to know I could leave my seat to buy a hotdog, take a leak, or visit with a friend, and I wouldn't miss anything happening on the diamond. I didn't even complain when it took thirty minutes to change pitchers.

At the Big U., the only thing reminiscent of those days is our seventy-two-year-old baseball coach, Grady McNutt. Grady once did a stint in the show, and he loves talking about it. He chews tobacco instead of bubble gum or sunflower seeds. Chew is against NCAA rules now—stupid, if you ask me—but I let Grady sneak around and do it.

Only Grady would complain when I ordered carpet for his office. "There's nowhere to spit," he said.

Baseball is a non-revenue sport at most universities. While an athletic director likes to see all of his teams do well, baseball was a particular breather for me. Nothing was expected of the program. It was a work in progress when I arrived here, and it still is.

Most people don't know that college baseball is a half-scholarship sport. The NCAA limits you to twelve a year. You'd have to be a Ted Williams popped up out of the grave to receive a full ride. Which is why most coaches try to recruit kids whose families are able to pick up half the tab for their tuition.

We have another excuse. Our winters are too long. It would be a miracle if the Big U. ever made it to the College World Series in Omaha. The warm-climate schools have a big edge in winning their conferences and surviving the regionals and super-regionals to punch a ticket to Omaha.

Frequent Omaha visitors like Southern Cal, Texas, LSU, Miami, Arizona State, and Stanford are practicing baseball in January and February while our guys are having snowball fights. It's not surprising that a Big 10 team hasn't won the College World Series in over fifty years.

Grady says you can't make it to the Elite Eight in Omaha unless you bring the Big Uglies with you. One would be the money slugger. The guy with a psychotic hatred of pitchers who can give you the winning hit in a late inning.

This guy stands in the box and glares at the pitcher and says, "Gimme your best shot, piss-hat. What's it gonna be? Your backdoor slider? Your four-seamer? Don't matter. When it leaves my bat, it ain't comin' down till it's somewhere over Iowa."

The other Big Uglies you need are on the hill. It takes two to win in Omaha. Two hurlers who stand six six, weigh 270, are twenty-seven years old, truth be known, and don't throw nothing but Tylenol.

In Grady's thirty years at the Big U., he's only had one player make it to the show. That was Potato Head Myers, an outfielder. Potato Head had an exceptional rookie season with the Pittsburgh Pirates, but injuries of one kind or another ruined the rest of his career. Potato Head possessed a world of talent, but hustle and practice weren't among his finest qualities. Injuries haunted him, and his five seasons in the majors were spent in a downward spiral with four other clubs.

Potato Head ended up as a utility man with the Texas Rangers in his last season and departed with a nickname given to him by a Dallas seamhead—baseball writer. It was "King of the Hamstrings."

Grady came in my office one morning to say he'd found out what Potato Head Myers was doing now. After working at odd jobs, he was now living in Florida and working as a toll booth operator on the Boca Grande Causeway.

Grady said, "I knew he'd wind up with a job in the shade."

Grady's biggest fan on the campus is L.M. "Lunch Meat" Duncan, our dogged director of sports information. Lunch Meat is the most rabid baseball fan I've ever known. Major league baseball is his favorite sport, his hobby, his obsession, his religion.

All it takes to know this is to look around in his office and his garage at home. You'll see stacks of newspapers everywhere. They're back copies of *The Sporting News*. Lunch Meat's granddaddy started collecting them in the early 1920s. His granddad was a passionate baseball fan and *The Sporting News* was the weekly bible of the game. He bequeathed his collection to Lunch Meat's dad, who continued to buy and save the issues from the 1930s through 1957. Those copies now belong to Lunch Meat.

His dad stopped the collection after the '57 season when the Brooklyn Dodgers and New York Giants moved to the west coast. This was the tragic end of baseball as we know it, he said. Los Angeles wasn't for baseball. Los Angeles was for golf, tennis, and movie stars. San Francisco wasn't for baseball. San Francisco was for bridges, Alcatraz, and cable cars.

Lunch Meat now owns thirty-five years of old copies of *The Sporting News*, and he takes his time reading them, refusing to skip ahead.

I would check with him to see what was going on in his baseball world. I recall the day he was caught up in the season of 1934. The St. Louis Cardinals, "the Gas House Gang," were going to meet the vaunted Detroit Tigers in the World Series.

"I love these Cardinals," Lunch Meat said. "You gotta love a team with guys named Dizzy Dean, Pepper Martin, Ducky Medwick, and Ripper Collins. The Tigers look pretty awesome themselves with Hank Greenberg, Mickey Cochrane, Charlie Gehringer, Goose Goslin, and Schoolboy Rowe on the mound. It ought to be a great World Series."

I said, "Let me know how it comes out."

"Oh, I will," he said excitedly.

Lunch Meat could sit at the feet of Grady and talk baseball for hours. I'd join them occasionally and listen to them discuss such earth-shaking subjects as, well, the bunt. Lunch Meat was no fan of the bunt. It was a sign of weakness. The flip side of manhood. He particularly disliked the bunt with a runner on first. Why give up an out to advance a man to second? Why not get a hit? That way you have two men on base and *nobody* out.

Grady spit a stream of chew, and said, "You may have something there, Lunchie. I should have mentioned that to my skipper Ralph Houk when the Yankees brought me up from Richmond."

Grady spent his twelve years in the show with the New York Yankees, but unfortunately they were among the worst years in Yankee history. He arrived there in the spring of 1966 as a utility outfielder and hung on long enough to get a ring when the Yankees made a comeback to win the World Series in 1977 under Manager Billy Martin.

This was the Yankee team of Reggie Jackson, Graig Nettles, Thurman Munson, Mickey Rivers, and Ron Guidry. They lit up the Empire State Building for the first time in fifteen years. Longest nightmare in modern Yankee history.

Lunch Meat would make Grady tell the same stories over and over. Some of them concerned immortals that Grady knew during his stay in the majors. Mickey Mantle, for one.

"Mick is the greatest ballplayer that ever lived who was never in shape," Grady said. "Think what he'd have done on two legs. He was a funny guy, too, even when he wasn't trying to be."

Funny like the day Mantle overheard two teammates in the dugout discussing a story in the news about a pro football player who'd been arrested for exposing himself to a teenage girl.

Mickey said, "I didn't know that was against the law."

Funny like the time Mickey wanted to celebrate moving from a junior suite into the presidential suite at the Essex House Hotel across from Central Park, where he lived during his best years with the Yankees. Mantle had lusted after the presidential suite, but it wasn't available—Charles Laughton, the actor, lived there permanently. But one day Mantle invited Grady and other teammates to come to the hotel bar that night. He was throwing a party to celebrate moving into the presidential suite.

Somebody said, "Mickey, Charles Laughton's not dead."

Mantle, "No, but he's bad sick."

■ ▣ ▣

ANOTHER immortal was Don Drysdale. Grady's first time at bat against Drysdale was memorable. It came in a spring training game in Vero Beach between the Yankees and Dodgers.

Miraculously, Grady laced a triple into centerfield on his first trip up. But as he stood on the third base bag proudly adjusting his cap he was suddenly surprised to see Drysdale walking over to him.

Drysdale, famous for his lethal sidearm fastball, arrived and said, "What's your name, kid?"

Grady said, "I'm Grady McNutt."

Drysdale said, "Well, I'm Don Drysdale. You know you have to go down, don't you?"

■ ▣ ▣

TODAY I've grown to like baseball lore and baseball stats more than I like baseball. I do follow the major league races. But through the years I've learned that if the game was as complicated as sportswriters and sportscasters make it out to be, baseball players couldn't play it.

THIRTY ONE

I ONCE read a quote in a magazine by a guy in Texas who said, "The only thing worse than track is field."

I laughed at it then, and I laugh at it now. But I confess I'm a closet fan of the sport. Even two of the field events, the pole vault and high jump. However, I do question the legitimacy of the heights they achieve these days.

Tell me this. Could the guy who holds the world record in the pole vault really try to sail over a bar twenty feet high, and could the guy who holds the world record in the high jump really try to clear a bar eight feet high if—just consider this—if they didn't have a big thick mattress to land on?

I'm not saying they ought to land on gravel. But I do wonder how high they'd try to go if they had to come down in one of the old shallow sand pits of yesteryear. Would it be worth a broken shoulder?

I'm not suggesting that any of that is the reason track and field has gradually been swept out of the nation's sports pages— except every four years when the Summer Olympics rolls around.

The Summer Olympics was great fun in the days when the USA and Russia were trying to out-hero each other in a culture war. But as we thought then, better in a sports stadium than with hydrogen bombs, right? Things are different now. There's no more Soviet Union. It's broken up into Kackystans and Ubeckystans, or whatever. Russia isn't Russia anymore in sports, not without their juiced-up athletes, and this has contributed to the slump in interest.

But what's done more damage to track and field coverage is the spread of pro sports. A bunch of states now have two major sports teams, some have three, and a dozen or more plus the District of Columbia have the whole alphabet: MLB, NFL, NBA, and NHL. Yeah, even ice hockey. A sport that largely benefits the dental industry.

Today you're lucky if you can find the results of a major track meet in the small type of a paper. If so, that news will be buried between the results of a meaningless tennis match in Gstaad and the fishing reports from Turkeyfoot Lake.

We'd done poorly in track and field for years, but nobody bothered to care since it was a non-revenue sport. I decided to do something about it five years ago out of nothing but pride.

My first move was to send our longtime track coach, Shorty Dawson, out to graze. The best thing Shorty did was take a guy to the Drake Relays where he accidentally finished third in the 5,000-meter run after half the field collapsed from asthma attacks.

Shorty was coach of the women's track team as well, not that he paid any attention to it. We were always fresh out of Flo-Jos. Shorty did have two decent lady competitors. One was Cherry Gooch, who put the shot, tossed the discus, and was undefeated in cake-eating contests. The other was a human skeleton, Monica Page, a distance runner who continually jogged around the campus, day and night. All Shorty did in the way of coaching was watch Monica run past him, and holler, "Buy a dress!"

For her funeral, he meant, after she died of starvation.

I sent Shorty to the campus maintenance crew and hired Coach Billy Tilly, a smooth-talking black dude. He had made a name for himself by turning Tennessee AR&N's track team into a locomotive. I sent Billy down to Jamaica with a pocketful of scholarships, and told him to recruit every kid he saw who could run a ten-flat hundred, uphill, in the rain, with a stolen computer under his arm.

I sometimes say things like that to see if I can give a coughing fit to a politically correct disciple. It's a hobby.

Billy said our way out of the wilderness was to recruit speed. Build the team around the dashes and relays. Ignore the weight events, he said, which required recruiting athletes from Samoa.

He made a neat haul on his first trip to Jamaica, and he's been going back since. The Big U. became an empire of speed. Billy's first recruits from Jamaica were four Bob Marleys and two other guys. You never stop learning things. I didn't know Bob Marley was a common first name in Jamaica.

Now our track team was led by the speedsters Bob Marley Clarke, Bob Marley Campbell, Bob Marley Gray, and Bob Marley Green. The other two recruits were Lennox Cook and Buju Malcolm, two athletes who specialized in the 400-meter dash. They combined to earn us a nickname that Lunch Meat Duncan proudly came up with: The Flying Cheetahs.

Billy Tilly went back to Kingston and brought us Jay-Jay Gordon, a highly sought competitor in the long jump, which used to be called the broad jump, and a wiry fellow named Antwan Larry, a specialist in the triple jump, which used to be called the hop, step, and jump.

Our recruiting efforts made us favored for the team title four years ago when we went to Eugene, Oregon, for the NCAA National Outdoor Championships. I invited Glenda to come along with Rita Jo and me, suggesting there might be some interesting golf courses in the area she could play if she didn't want to watch the track meet every day. She passed, saying she never enjoyed playing golf in a rubber suit. I took that to be a comment on Oregon weather.

Our fans were excited about the prospect of winning the Big U.'s first national championship in any sport. When you're going after the team title in track, the points are awarded in an event like this: 10-8-6-5-4-3-2-1. That's 10 for the winner and on down. It's only fair that the athlete should receive one point at least for finishing eighth after surviving the grueling prelims to reach the finals. Total up the most points scored by a school in the final events and you have the team champion.

For four days in Eugene it was a slugfest between us and the Florida Gators, who had won the nationals twice. The Gators dominated the weight and field events and racked up points in the distances. We ruled the speed, starting with our four Bob Marleys—Clarke, Campbell, Gray, and Green.

They won the 4x100-meter relay, once known as the speed relay, in a time of 38.5, which would have been a world record a decade ago. Three of the Bob Marleys—Gray, Green, and Campbell—followed up the relay triumph by placing second, third, and fifth in the 100-meter dash.

We scored well again in the 200-meter dash when Bob Marley Clarke and Bob Marley Campbell took second and fourth. Our quartermilers came through for us in the 400-meter dash as Lennox Cook grabbed third and Buju Malcolm fourth.

We scratched out enough points in three other events to keep the heat on Florida. With one event to go, we trailed Florida by one point, 49 to 50, but fate left us with a golden opportunity. The last event was the 4x400 relay, once the mile relay. We made the finals but Florida didn't. We were practically given the title.

Rita Jo said, "Are we good-enough people to deserve this?"

I said, "You are. I'm not sure about me."

Our 4x400 relay foursome of Lennox Cook, Buju Malcolm, Bob Marley Clarke, and Bob Marley Campbell hadn't lost a race in two years. They could sleep-walk through the race and finish no worse than third. But we didn't need third. We only needed to place seventh, worth two points. This would be good enough to wrap up the team title by one point over Florida. If there was ever a mortal lock, it was us.

We went down on the infield and listened in as Coach Billy Tilly gave our relay team his final instructions. "We don't need to win this race," he said. "We've got the national championship in our hands. Think about that ring you'll be proud to wear the rest of your lives. Keep it on cruise control. Make sure to pass the stick in your zone. Stay clear of the pack. Don't get tripped up. I know you want to win the race, but we don't need to win this race. We need to finish fifth, sixth, seventh, and that'll be the biggest win of your career. Okay? Let's go get it."

Before the eight lead-off runners took to their blocks, Coach Billy and I were being congratulated by other coaches and ADs. Even Florida's coach, Skeezix Frailey, was congratulating me.

The first 400 meters was a breeze. Lennox Cook gave us a seven-yard lead without pushing it. He handed the baton off to Buju Malcolm and Buju increased the lead to ten yards, leaving the pack behind. He passed the baton to Bob Marley Clarke, who easily stretched the lead to fifteen yards. I don't mind admitting it was embarrassing when Bob Marley Clarke sprinted down the last one hundred meters flashing a big smile and waving at the crowd.

Then it happened.

If I hadn't seen it with my own eyes, Rita Jo would have alerted me to it when she yelled out, "Oh, for God's sake!"

Either Bob Marley Clarke botched the hand-off to Bob Marley Campbell, or Bob Marley Campbell accidentally dropped the stick when Bob Marley Clarke tried to hand it to him. Whatever the screw-up, the baton bounced around on the track as the two Bob Marleys cussed and threw clavicle shots at each other and impeded two runners trying to pass them and knocked down another one. Our relay team was instantly disqualified. Red flags waved everywhere.

We would collect no points in the event—and Western Ohio University's first national championship had been flushed down a commode in the most unexpected way imaginable.

I was dazed. I felt like the Alien had suddenly busted out of a stranger's chest and devoured my relay team.

I was left to wander around in the infield and shake my head and feel sorry for the rest of our team as I forced a weak smile and accepted condolences from the other coaches, officials, and athletic directors.

Coach Billy Tilly's reaction was different. He stomped on his ballcap, and plunked down on the grass and wept. But when the Bob Marleys moved their argument to the infield, the coach stood up and glared at them, his rage growing.

Rita Jo and I moved over next to Billy and listened to the Bob Marleys blame the loss on each other as their relay teammates, Lennox Cook and Buju Malcolm, jumped in and blamed both of them. As the four of them pushed, shoved, and yelled at one another, we overheard:

"You drop de stick, mon!"

"No, you s'pose to grab de stick."

"Grab my bumba!"

"Both you foul up, mon."

"You kiss mi pecker nub."

"Folk you, batty boy!"

"Mi rass, you."

"Batty boy you talk!"

"Next time I put de stick up your ass, mon!"

"*Next time!*" Coach Billy hollered, throwing himself into the middle of their dust-up. They stopped to stare at him.

Billy said, "*What* next time? What did I tell you? *What the fuck did I say to you before the race? We don't need to win the race!* We need to win the national championship. That's what I said, you ignorant bastards. You could *stand still* and hand off the baton and we'd be national champions. Look what you cost us, you stupid-ass calypso, day-O, reggae, limbo-loving . . ." And on into the curry goat and fish tea.

■ ■ ■

LAST YEAR it was with a considerable amount of pride and joy that I watched TV as Bob Marley Clarke and Bob Marley Campbell heaped glory on both Jamaica and Western Ohio University at the Summer Olympics in Jakarta. They sped to a one-two finish in the final of the 200-meter dash—the gold medal for Bob Marley Clarke, the silver for Bob Marley Campbell. It was gratifying to see them take the lead on the curve and hold on to the tape.

And a day later it was pretty doggone exciting to watch on TV as they both outran the killer tsunami that flooded the north end of Java.

THIRTY TWO

YOU COULD call it long overdue progress or you could just call it expensive. I refer to Title IX, the big Roman numeral in college sports.

While Title IX may have been necessary in the progress of mankind, or I should say womankind, it has come close to turning more than one athletic director into a math wonk.

I'm not sure I'd have stayed employed at Western Ohio if the university hadn't been taken into the Big 10 and showered with TV money for having a competitive football team. That money helped me pay for the scholarships I've provided for the athletes who compete in our non-rev sports—track and field, baseball, golf, tennis, swimming and diving, softball, soccer, beach volleyball, rifle, and equestrian.

The Big U. now has more NCAA sports for women than it does for men. And yet it's a given that the athletic director who replaces me will hear a mysterious voice behind him whispering, "Be on the lookout for . . . archery . . . crew . . . lacrosse . . . gymnastics . . . field hockey . . . water polo . . . rugby . . ."

Did I leave out fencing?

How is the poor guy going to finance those sports in addition to what I've left on his plate? Hold a bake sale?

The Title IX law, passed in 1972, says that every college must provide equal opportunity and resources for women in sports or face the possibility of being denied federal funds for sports or any other educational use.

My predecessor, lovable Amos Alonzo Howell, ignored Title IX. He refused to believe the law applied to private universities. Amos was on record saying, "Women ain't supposed to go running and jumping around. Women is supposed to shell peas and fold laundry."

He did consider putting in women's golf and tennis on the basis that they were country club sports. He said, "Women with good manners should be allowed to compete in these gentlemanly games."

But he left it for me to do after he passed the torch.

Amos tolerated swimming and diving while claiming that America never should have let those sports escape from summer camp. He wondered if swimming and diving would ever have become collegiate sports if Johnny Weissmuller hadn't splashed his way to stardom at the '24 Olympics in Paris and gone on to become Tarzan in the movies.

Carter Bailey, our swimming and diving coach, a prematurely gray fellow who'd maintained a trim build at the age of fifty-six, has been here for twenty-five years but his swimmers have never won a team title. He's coached his share of individual medal winners. A freestyler here, a backstroker there.

The rules of swimming and diving baffle me. I've never understood why an athlete is allowed to win five medals for swimming the same distance five times. And I'm convinced that the judges who score dives tend to base their marks on how close the athletes come to bumping their heads on the springboard or the platform when they start down after leaping up to begin the dive.

I say these things about swimming and diving while acknowledging that Michael Phelps was a once-in-a-lifetime athlete. They ought to name a candy bar after him.

I left Carter Bailey's program alone, much to his satisfaction—and mine.

But I'll never forget the morning he came in my office as Rita Jo and I were busy discussing travel plans or something. He asked if I could spare a scholarship or even two for him to add synchronized swimming as a competitive event.

"For men or women?" I asked.

Carter didn't understand my grin, I was certain.

He said, "I don't know if men do it, Pete."

I said, "Well, if you don't, I sure don't."

Rita Jo chimed in, and said, "Carter, I would love to see you add synchronized swimming for the ladies—and I know how to make the event more exciting than it seems to be today."

Carter said, "You do?"

Rita Jo said, "Yeah. Throw a toaster in the pool."

It took a long moment for her remark to sink in on Carter. At which point he manufactured a weak smile and bent over and put his palms together and apologetically backed out of the office.

THIRTY THREE

IT DIDN'T surprise anyone in my department that forty years after Title IX became the law of the land a survey by a sports foundation revealed that 80 percent of America's universities were still failing to comply.

Rita Jo reacted to the survey as only she could.

She said, "I see where the state schools are still counting thirty girls in a rowing shell that only seats eight."

But Title IX didn't have as much to do with me adding softball and soccer to our women's scholarship load as a board member did. The twin daughters of a wealthy board member were ready to enter college and they'd always dreamed of playing softball and soccer at the Big U.

Bartle Crumby was the board member. He had done so well in the insurance business that when the twin girls were born he named them Fire and Casualty. Their mother, Veronica, had no say in the matter—Bartle was too rich for anybody to argue with him on any subject. The girls did receive permission from dad to change their names in high school to Fear and Cass.

I added the two sports when Bartle volunteered to pay for the softball and soccer stadiums if the university would purchase the land. A desirable piece of land for expansion was across the street from the far edge of the campus, a neighborhood of old Victorian homes, some of which had reached tear-down stage.

The university offered to buy the entire neighborhood for a sum the board thought was reasonable, but the owners accused the board of trying to steal their homes. They formed an association and hired a lawyer. University trustees cuss out loud when this happens.

The purchase price soared to $600,000 per house, and there were fifteen houses. The total came to $8.3 million. And that wasn't the end of it. Four of the homes were occupied by owners who demanded to be relocated. They wanted to go to a gated community in Scottsdale, Arizona, that advertised a lake for fishing and boating, a shopping village with a variety of restaurants, and two eighteen-hole golf courses.

When I presented their demands to the board, I tried to soften the blow with humor. I said, "My wife says to tell the homeowners to wait till she grabs her clubs and she'll go with them."

The trustees gasped and moaned but made the purchase and the school now has state-of-the-art softball and soccer stadiums that are nicely landscaped and hold 3,000 fans each—if that many fans ever show up.

Fear Crumby made the starting softball lineup at first base, and in her freshman season led the team in home runs with three. Bartle never missed a home game and frequently offered suggestions to the umpires that could be heard from six rows away.

The coach I hired for softball was Suzanne Dudley. Rita Jo found her on the Net. Suzanne came from a small college near Gloucester, Massachusetts, and was excited to be coaching at a place where every other game wouldn't be cancelled by a perfect storm.

I was joking when I asked Suzanne to make sure her girls didn't dogpile on the diamond every time somebody got a hit. Better to hold off on that sort of display until they win a game or even a tournament.

Suzanne Dudley said, "Don't worry about it, Mr. Wallace. I'll try not to recruit too many ladies who've been overexposed to foreign films."

I liked that woman. I knew I'd made a good hire.

◾ ◾ ◾

THE SOCCER coach was another good hire. This was Molly Brewster's first coaching job, but she came with an impressive resume. She's been a defender on the USA national teams that won the Olympic gold as well as the world championship. Two of her former teammates and international stars, Julie Foudy and Mia Hamm, wrote letters on her behalf, as did the CEO of Clabber Girl Baking Powder in her hometown of Terre Haute, Indiana.

"I hope you're going to be patient," Molly said. "Success in soccer doesn't happen overnight. You have to start recruiting girls when they're 12 and 13, and keep working on them until you sign them for college."

I said, "Molly, you're in charge. Like most American men, it's hard for me to understand a sport where nobody falls on a loose ball."

She frowned.

"Humor," I explained.

People who brag about understanding soccer have assured me there's a science to it. I take their word for it. All I know is, every time I watch a game on TV, whether it's between men or women, I never see a goal scored that doesn't appear to be a complete accident.

Even the penalty kick is a fluke. I would ask the world to rethink the penalty kick. The distance is too short. The poor goalie either guesses right or wrong. If the goalie guesses right in a World Cup game, say, the goalie becomes a legend for life. But if the goalie guesses wrong, he or she is consigned to a lifetime of humiliation, forced to wear a disguise and move in the shadows.

It's worse if the goalie is a guy. Punishment seems to differ on the continents. In the romantic countries of Europe—France, Italy, Spain, Portugal—the goalie who costs his nation a championship will be hounded by fans and the media until he's changed his name, had surgery, and become a transgender.

But in Latin American countries, where the sport of soccer dominates all other news including wars, military coups, and the comings and goings of Evitas, the fans are more emotional.

Take Argentina, Brazil, or one of the Uruguays. Down there, the goalie who costs his team a championship is abruptly beheaded. His head is placed on a stick and paraded around the stadium in front of the blood-thirsty crowd—right up until part of the stadium collapses and another 120 people perish.

In an effort to put our soccer coach at ease in the job, I asked Molly Brewster if I could pass along a piece of advice in regard to recruiting.

She said, "I'll take all the help I can get. The girls I've inherited are awfully slow, and they don't take criticism too well. Cass Crumby in particular. When I told her she only has one foot, she pouted for a week."

I said I was aware of the task she'd taken on, and that was why I wanted to suggest that when she goes scouting for talent, she ought to consider spending a little time down along the Texas-Mexico border.

I said, "Check out the illegal aliens that come flying past you. I mean, you know the sumbitches can *run*."

THIRTY FOUR

BRILLIANT, I called it. Simply brilliant. I speak of the appeal I made to the board's sense of patriotism when I wanted to add equestrian and rifle to our lineup of women's sports.

You have to consider the timing. This was two years ago when the majority of Americans wanted to grab every A-rab they could reach and tell him to knock off this terrorist shit or we'd make his desert glow in the dark.

When I appeared before the board I asked the members to name the two things that had made America the greatest country in the world.

Clarence Fischer, lumber company bobblehead, said, "Icebox and air-conditioning?"

I shook my head, *no*.

W.C. Becker, roofing bobblehead, said, "Law and order?"

I said, "It was a good idea. I wish we still had some."

Curtis Abernathy, strip mall bobblehead, said, "Boats and cars?"

I said, "May I give you the answer?"

Chancellor Carpenter said, "Yes, if you don't mind, Pete."

"Horses and guns," I said proudly.

Everybody stared at me.

I said, "If it hadn't been for horses and guns we wouldn't have won any wars from George Washington to Sergeant York.

We wouldn't have blazed the trails that made America grow and prosper and invent college football. And we'd still be chasing Geronimo on foot with rocks and pointed sticks."

That should have brought a laugh, but didn't.

I said, "Horses and guns are patriotic sports when you think about it. Horses and guns . . . equestrian and rifle."

"Rifle and *what*?" Clarence Fischer said.

"E-quess-tree-un," I said slowly. "That's what they call the sport that's played on horses. There are two disciplines. There's Hunt Seat, where the girls dress like English ladies and jump horses over fences, and there's Western Style, where the girls play cowboy and make horses spin around in circles, stop and go, slide, trot, jog, and prance."

Everybody stared at me again.

I looked at Roy Clapper and said, "Your ranch south of town has a cutting horse arena. We could build grandstands and use it for our equestrian team's home field and training site. "

Roy said, "We could—if you convince me it'll be worth it."

I said, "Roy, I want to win a national championship here in *something*. I like the odds in equestrian and rifle. Not that many schools compete in the NCAA's first division. It's not like having to beat the whole world to win it all in basketball."

Roy asked, "What's the competition?"

I said, "In equestrian, mostly Southern schools. Oklahoma State, South Carolina, Georgia, TCU, Auburn. Another thing about equestrian, you can win the nationals in Overall, Western, or Hunt Seat. You have three chances."

Roy asked, "How many scholarships does it take?"

I said, "You're allowed fifteen for equestrian, ten for rifle. I'll find the money somewhere. And it'll help with Title IX. Equestrian and rifle will both be women's sports."

W.C. Becker said, "Them rifle teams don't shoot at each other, do they?"

I said, "They shoot at targets, W.C. One team against another. They shoot small bore—a twenty-two—and air rifle. In small bore, the target's fifty feet. In air rifle, it's thirty yards. Eight teams make it to the national finals and knock off one another till the last two meet for the championship."

Curtis Abernathy said, "Those distances sound easy."

I said, *"Easy?* Curtis, the target's the size of a *flea*."

Roy said, "Where do we find athletes and coaches for these sports?"

I said, "Rita Jo's on it."

My closer.

■ ■ ■

THE COACH Rita Jo found for equestrian was Bunny Pemberton. She'd been the coach at the University of North Virginia until the school canceled the program for lack of funds.

Bunny Pemberton was eager to accept the job and said she'd bring her best prospects with her from Northern Virginia. They'd be the core of our Hunt Seat lineup. But she was honest enough to confess that she knew very little about coaching Western Style.

Rita Jo said, "That won't be a problem for you. The Western riders will come from wealthy ranch families in Texas, Wyoming, and Montana. These girls will have been on saddles since birth."

Bunny said, "I'll have to travel out west to recruit these girls?"

Rita Jo said, "We'll put you in jeans and a Stetson, and Pete can teach you how to talk country in no time. You won't have to coach the girls when they get here. They'll know horsemanship and they'll be too rich to listen to you anyway."

I made a fool of myself at the first meet I attended at Roy's ranch. The Oklahoma State girls had come to town to do battle with our Lady Cheetahs. The first chance I had, I stood up and punched my fist in the air and yelled, "Way to go, girl!" It looked like our rider had performed skillfully.

Then I realized I'd made the only sound in the grandstand. Everybody was gaping at me with what I took to be disgust.

A lady sitting in a row below me turned around and explained that in equestrian competition, you're not supposed to cheer. You're supposed to make a low, humming noise.

"Like this," she said, and made a soft "woo-woo" sound.

I put it on my to-do list.

We won the Western Style nationals the second year of the program. The meet was held in Blythewood, South Carolina, home field of the University of South Carolina Gamecocks. Our team consisted of Destiny Wilson from the Flying C in West Texas, Callie Cooper from the Four 8s in Oklahoma, Haley Clay from the Leaning Gate in Wyoming, and Kylee Parker from the Rocking R in Montana.

Destiny, our captain, said, "This was easier than gettin' on the outside of a chicken-fried steak. We'd have won this by more if they'd had barrel racing. You can believe *that* or kiss my leather seat."

Love a competitor.

■ ■ ■

KARINA VOLKOV, a native of Russia, was the coach Rita Jo found to lead our rifle team. Karina was born in Moscow but spoke perfect English. She'd been raised in the United States from the age of three. Her father, an ex-sniper in the Russian army, had moved the family to our shores when he inherited his grandfather's thriving caviar business in New York City.

Karina was sent to the best private schools in Manhattan, and she'd become a marksman by competing with her daddy at shooting birds and pigeons and empty cans of beer and V8 on the rooftop of their apartment building in Manhattan.

She received a scholarship in rifle at the University of Southeast Kentucky, where she won the individual nationals twice, and later became an assistant rifle coach at the school.

Karina was eager for a head coaching job. She assured Rita Jo that she could recruit shooters that would bring Western Ohio a national title. I couldn't resist asking Karina if it was true that ladies nowadays were proving to be as good, if not better, than the men at target shooting.

She said, "We have more nerve and better concentration. The mind of a man can wander—often to women, yes? We ladies know how to keep our eye on the target. This is a fact."

Karina's first six recruits were the steely-eyed Petra Azarov, the sharp-shooting Tatiana Dobrymin, the steady Grisha Popov, the calm Suzy Chang, the reliable Cynthia Hedgecroft, and the determined Olga Klus.

I asked the coach where she found those stalwarts.

Karina said, "All six come from United Nations families in New York. But don't worry, Pete. Only three of them are spies."

That Karina. Funny lady.

Now that I'd brought the sport to our campus, I was anxious to observe our team practicing so I'd become familiar with the competition. They set up targets in the hoops dome—college rifle is an indoor sport, I discovered, and Roy Clapper Coliseum was our home field.

I watched our girls practice under championship conditions. This called for each girl to shoot sixty rounds of small bore, stop and rest for no more than an hour, and then shoot sixty rounds of air rifle.

As Karina had promised, we became successful right off. After our twelve-match schedule, home and away, against the likes of Ohio State, TCU, The Citadel, Memphis, and Ole Miss, we were ranked No. 3 in the nation, and qualified as one of the eight teams to reach the finals.

The championship was held in Fort Benning, Georgia, at the United States Army Marksmanship Center. I watched with immense pride as Western Ohio upset Kentucky and West Virginia to reach the finals against West Point, the favorite.

Karina sent what she thought were her four best girls—Petra and Tatiana, the Russians; Suzy, the Chinese; and Cynthia, the Brit—to go up against the four top senior cadets for Army, whose names were Buzz, Dutch, Ace, and Spider.

Our ladies won.

Yes. They beat Army. West Point's finest sharpshooters.

I enjoyed hoisting the trophy for photo ops, but there was one thing troublesome about the result. It didn't fill me with overwhelming confidence in our nation's military preparedness.

THIRTY FIVE

WHEN I decided to install women's golf as an NCAA sport, Rita Jo said Glenda would be greatly pleased and it would give her an opportunity to renew her marriage vows to me. "Maybe so," I said, "but only after I listen to her birdies and bogeys of the day."

I added women's tennis at the same time, but Glenda ignores tennis. She says tennis is badminton on steroids. I hold the sport in a little higher regard than that, especially if I think about the careers of Rod Laver and Steffi Graf.

Men's golf and tennis had existed at the Big U. since the 1920s, but the only progress the guys made in tennis was to go from long pants to short pants, and all the golfers did was go from hickory shafts to steel.

Golf and tennis weren't even coached by professionals then. They were overseen by assistant professors who'd accompany the athletes to tournaments but use the time to grade papers and smoke cigarettes.

I figured it would be difficult to hire coaches for both sports because of our facilities. Pitiful would be the nicest thing you could say about them. We had no college golf course like Stanford, Yale, Ohio State, Michigan, and others. Pine Knot Golf Club was the only public course in town, and was largely known for its lack of a watering system and the retired geezers who showed up every day and took seven hours to play eighteen holes to avoid going home and having their wives drag them to the mall.

As for tennis, there were only four asphalt courts at the Big U. and they were surrounded by a tall wire fence and were relentlessly strewn with dead leaves. They looked like Prison Rec.

My first move was to talk Bent Oak into letting our golf and tennis teams use the club for practice. The classy surroundings would give our athletes a sense of pride. I assured the Board of Governors that our scholar-athletes would stay out of the way of the members when they were on the golf course, the range, the putting green, and the tennis courts.

Finding coaches was the next chore. I wanted a tennis coach who'd be in charge of both the women and the men's teams. I offered the job as a sideline to Denny Collins, the tennis pro at Bent Oak, but he said he was too busy.

I'd never noticed Denny being that busy on the courts. He must have meant busy servicing adventurous wives among the membership. Denny was a good-looking dude in his thirties, and I should have remembered that various male members referred to him as "Mule Dick."

I called on my fellow athletic directors for recommendations and wound up hiring Rodrigo Silva as our tennis coach. Rodrigo looked like the dashing but cocky bandit in an old cowboy movie who would be easily outdrawn in a gunfight. Rita Jo thought he looked more like the guy who shakes the *maracas* in a Latin orchestra. He had once ranked No. 94 in the world on the ATP tour, but after examining his cloudy future as a competitor, he turned to coaching and served two years as assistant tennis coach at the University of Miami. From there, he lucked into a job as the personal coach of Anastasia Belyakov, child star, age fourteen, daughter of a wealthy Russian businessman.

Rodrigo coached Anastasia for three years at one of the family homes in Naples, Florida. The property included three practice courts—grass, clay, and hard court—and a guest cottage for Rodrigo.

It was a plush job except that Rodrigo was informed by Anastasia's father that he expected his daughter to win the Wimbledon singles title by the age of eighteen or he would be "very disappointed."

Rodrigo resigned after Anastasia turned seventeen. He'd discovered that her father in reality was a wealthy Russian gangster, and Rodrigo didn't want to wait around to find out how disappointed a Russian gangster would be when his daughter failed to win Wimbledon by the age of eighteen, which she had no living chance to do.

On Rodrigo's first day on the job I said I didn't expect any miracles from him, but if I heard that he'd put his hands on any of the girls, I'd kick his Mediterranean ass back to Barcelona.

Last I checked, he was doing okay. He was impressed with a lad who seemed capable of returning a drop shot without breaking his ankle. And he was working with a young girl who showed potential if he could redirect her serve from an underhand lob to an overhead smash.

■ ■ ■

I ASSUMED it would please Glenda if I made Charlie Stall the head coach of both the men's and women's golf teams. They'd be practicing at Bent Oak, and it wasn't like Charlie was overworked. Most of his time was spent giving my wife playing lessons—or taking her to lunch or dinner.

I assumed wrong.

Glenda charged into my office to insist that Charlie be appointed head coach of the men, and she, Glenda Boyd Wallace, be appointed head coach of the women—with Charlie as her assistant.

Glenda further stunned me by saying that each of them should be paid a hundred and fifty grand a year.

I said, "That's impossible, Glenda. First, this should be a labor of love for you. Second, I can't find that kind of money in my budget."

She said, "Don't give me that crap. I've watched you juggle the budget at home and hum a tune while you did it."

I said, "Do you realize I would have to take a couple of full scholarships away from two deserving young girls in other sports to pay your salaries?"

She said, "So . . . ?"

I said, "That wouldn't bother you?"

She said, "You want the short answer? Fuck. Them."

I said, "You can't mean that."

She said, "I can't? Let me put it this way in case you've forgotten how much golf means to me. Fuck you, too."

Rita Jo happened to enter my office as Glenda was reminding me of how much golf meant to her, and said, "This sounds like a jolly conversation."

As Rita Jo helped herself to a bottle of water out of my fridge, I said, "My wife is asking the impossible of this department."

Rita Jo said, "How so?"

Looking at Rita Jo, Glenda said, "I want one-fifty a year to coach women's golf, and the same for Charlie Stall to coach the men."

Rita Jo said, "We don't have it."

Glenda said, "You'll find it . . . and this has nothing to do with you, Rita."

Rita Jo said, "It has everything to do with me. I spend more time worrying about the budget than Pete does."

Glenda said, "I'll deal with you, then."

I stood up and said, "Good. I'll go have a cigar."

Glenda said, "Sit your butt back down."

I sat back down.

Rita Jo said, "I'm so lucky I got here in time for this."

Glenda said, "These salaries are the going rate today for the coach of a successful program. I intend to make ours successful. I know the pay used to be less when the season was shorter and the coach supplemented his or her income with summer camps. But times have changed."

Rita Jo said, "I'm not sure we can find the money to pay you and Charlie as much as seventy-five a year."

Glenda said, "I'm not here to negotiate, Rita."

Rita Jo glanced at me, and said, "You better handle this, boss. I'm inexperienced at marriage counseling."

Glenda said, "Cute, Rita."

I said, "We'll think about it, Glenda."

Glenda said, "While you're at it, think about this. I'm going to take this program big-time. That means it's going to cost more than you think. I plan to enter our girls in the best college tournaments in the country. Competing at that level will help them gain experience and confidence."

I said, "How do you expect to recruit against Duke, Stanford, Arizona State, USC—the powerhouse teams—for America's top junior girls?"

Glenda said, "I'm aware of what I'm up against. The computer will help me find gifted youngsters in Europe, Asia, South Africa, Australia. And when they get here, I will personally mold them into better players and strong competitors."

Rita Jo said, "I like your attitude, Glenda. It would be nice to have another winning program among the non-revs. Tell you what. If I can find a small bank to knock over, we'll do our best to make your salaries happen."

As Glenda was leaving, she said, "I'll take that as a yes. You've always been good at making things happen, Rita."

A moment after Glenda departed, Rita Jo looked at me, and said, "That was a compliment, yes? No? Maybe?"

I leaned back in my leather chair, closed my eyes, and said, "I'll have to check with Dr. Phil."

THIRTY SIX

I HAVE a piece of paper framed on my wall that says I'm an educated man. Never mind that my degree came from the Texas College of Fine Arts & Ranching. Therefore, as an educated man, I should have known what would happen to our charming English cottage if I named my wife coach of the women's golf team.

If I wanted to treat it lightly, I would describe it as a reenactment of a historic event. Our home played San Francisco, Glenda played the earthquake.

But it was gradual.

I watched our beautiful emerald front lawn of native Ohio fescue become a pitching range. I watched our beautiful emerald back lawn become a chipping range. But since the back lawn was fenced in, it continued to serve as a doggie playground for Marissa, the poodle, and Clive, the spaniel. They delighted in chasing the golf balls. Some hither, others yon.

I watched the front and back lawns become lit up by floodlights attached to the roof gutters and the limbs on our magnificent oak trees. And I also watched our wall-to-wall living-room carpet become a putting green while the living room sofas and chairs became a lounge for golfers only. While the transformation was underway, I chose a moment to ask Glenda if all of it was totally necessary.

She said, "Are you embarrassed by the flagsticks in the front yard?"

I said, "I wasn't until a neighbor asked me how much the greens fees are."

She said, "Tell him it's an exclusive private club, like the Augusta National."

I gave that the laugh it deserved.

She said, "If that doesn't work, tell him to bite my Titleist."

I said, "Do we really need the outdoor lighting, Glenda?"

She said, "Yes, of course. You've obviously never noticed that Bent Oak doesn't have lights on the practice range or putting green. My recruits are going to be devoting as many hours as possible to improving their games."

I said, "I never could have guessed it would include our home."

She said, "Consistent practice is how you build a winner. A winning golfer has to develop a swing that repeats under pressure."

I said, "Who said that first, you or some golf guy on TV?"

Her look indicated a response wasn't required.

I said, "Pardon me for forgetting the lights are necessary. I forgot your team will be competing in that many night tournaments."

She said, "Jokes are often a disguise for ignorance. I read that somewhere about Hollywood people."

I said, "Then you won't mind if I put a sign out by the curb."

She said, "You're going to put a sign on our street?"

I said, "For the people who drive by. It'll say, 'Honk If You Like Golf More Than Banana Pudding.'"

"Darn," she said. "I was hoping it would be funny."

Another thing. I watched every TV set in our house suddenly become deprived of news and movies in favor of golf instruction videos, including the set in my private office/den. That was where Charlie Stall most often liked to relax and watch the golf instruction DVDs he'd bring over.

I came home one evening and found him comfortably seated in my desk chair, having a Coors Light and watching *The Teeny Bikinis Do Golf.*

I browsed through the discs on my desk and noticed it came from a stack of Charlie's that included two other tantalizing titles: *Miley Cyrus Takes a Free Drop*, and *The Bogey Whisperer with Paulina Gretzky.*

I learned not to mind Charlie showing up with dinner for the two of them—Chinese takeout—on the average of three times a week, and the other evenings when he and Glenda would compete in a vicious putting contest on our living room carpet. Those evenings freed me up to take Rita Jo to dinner, where we would talk about anything but golf.

I would take her to the Town Club or Emily's Steakhouse or *Estupido Gringos*, the only Tex-Mex joint in town. It wasn't up to the standards of my home state, but if I was badly in need of an enchilada fix, I'd lap it up and say, "It's not very good . . . but isn't it good?"

Then we'd go back to discussing astrophysics.

THIRTY SEVEN

GLENDA'S first recruiting class consisted of five girls from five different countries, none of which happened to be the United States.

Cecile Bisson was from France, Kirski Lakso from Finland, Marta Nystrom from Sweden, Heidi Jung from Germany, and Ji-moo Park from South Korea. All of them spoke passable English, although the only thing I ever heard the South Korean say was, "You make joke."

Glenda couldn't have worked her girls harder if she'd taken a bullwhip to the Bent Oak practice range and a cattle prod to the putting green.

In the meantime, she tried to jam everything into their heads that she'd learned from studying the best golf instruction books ever written, which she insisted were those produced by Tommy Armour, Ben Hogan, Harvey Penick, and Jack Nicklaus.

There were scads of other instruction books on our shelves at home that were written by self-declared experts on the game even though their names were unfamiliar to most golf nuts. I was willing to wager that these authors had rewritten Armour, Hogan, Penick, and Nicklaus and, to be safe, had dropped in some wisdom from *Chicken Soup for the Soul*.

Since Charlie Stall didn't care about it, Glenda took it upon herself to make out the schedule for the men's team. They would only compete in tournaments in and around the Midwest. At a glance it looked like a nice savings for the department, but I knew what her ulterior motive was. More money to spend on the women's team.

The men traveled by bus to Bloomington, Madison, Ann Arbor, and other destinations accompanied by a student manager whose job it was to see that the young men found their way to the Days Inns reserved for them.

Glenda's team traveled differently. She arranged for her girls and their coach and assistant coach—Glenda and Charlie—to fly first class on major airlines and stay in luxury hotels.

The girls competed in a schedule that sent them to the most desirable women's tournaments and the annual Big 10 championship. Rita Jo had succeeded in carving Glenda's proposed schedule down from twenty events to fifteen. Still, Glenda made sure her team was invited to play in the two most exotic college tournaments, the Rio Mar Classic in Puerto Rico and the all-important Abalonie Cup on the Monterey Peninsula.

I say all-important because it meant the girls and the coaches would stay in the Pebble Beach Lodge, one of Glenda's cherished haunts.

Glenda's team achieved success sooner than I expected. I'd say Glenda and Charlie Stall's team except I was reasonably sure that Charlie's primary responsibility as assistant coach was to select the wines for dinner. There were positive signs their first season. The team finished fourth in the Silverado Showdown in Napa, California, and third in the Big 10 conference tournament at Oakland Hills Country Club near Detroit.

This season they were competitive in every event and won the Peachtree Cup in Atlanta. They were undoubtedly energized by staying at the Ritz-Carlton in Buckhead. If you don't live in the

Buckhead neighborhood of Atlanta, I learned from Janice Clapper and Rochelle Stoddard, you're supposed to commit suicide.

With their confidence and egos boosted by that victory, Glenda's girls stormed through the Big 10 championship at Interlachen Country Club in Minneapolis and edged out Purdue to win the conference title.

Glenda emailed me, "God, I love these girls."

Then it was on to the NCAA championship, their first trip in history. The NCAAs were held this time at North Shore Country Club in a suburb of Chicago.

Glenda reserved rooms for her girls and coaches at the exalted Drake Hotel during the week. A reward for the team's season. It enabled Glenda and Charlie to have tea as often as possible in the hotel's stylish Palm Court.

We were one of fifteen teams that qualified for the NCAAs. It first called for fifty-four holes of stroke play, and the eight teams with the lowest total scores would flail away at match play to decide the national championship.

Our girls took it in stride. They smoothly romped through the stroke-play qualifying, finished second, and won their first two rounds of match play with surprising upsets over Duke and Arizona State.

This put them in the finals against Stanford. Being of international origins, our ladies weren't intimidated by the big-name schools. They didn't know one from the other, and cared less. My guess was they considered college golf a mere stopover on their way to our LPGA Tour.

Rita Jo flew out to be on the scene for the finals. She thought the department should be represented in case we won. I would have gone with her, but if our team lost, I knew Glenda would blame me for it by jinxing them with my presence.

What transpired in the finals was reported to me later in detail by Rita Jo.

She walked the whole last day with Glenda and Charlie. They moved back and forth to keep up with the four matches.

The four competitors Glenda chose to do battle with Stanford were France's Cecile Bisson, Germany's Heidi Jung, Sweden's Marta Nystrom, and South Korea's Ji-moo Park. Stanford countered with four big strong girls who had shoulders like swimmers and legs like soccer players. They were all named Mary Alice Langford or something.

There's little a golf coach can do in the midst of a competition but watch nervously. It's against the rules to grab a girl and threaten to beat her into a concussion with a Great Big Bertha driver if she misses a fairway.

After Marta Nystrom crumbled under the pressure and quickly lost her match, the other three duels looked like they'd come down to the wire.

"Sweden," Glenda screeched. "What's it good for? Meatballs . . . fjords . . . guys named Sven . . . *what?*"

Then when the normally dependable Heidi Jung, the German lass, lipped out three straight short putts to surrender her lead and fall into a tie with her opponent, Glenda's anger got the best of her.

She blurted out to Charlie and Rita Jo, "Why in the name of God would I recruit a girl from a country where the people don't do anything but march in the streets, sing songs, drink beer, and never win a fucking war?"

The last three matches did, in fact, come down to the eighteenth hole. First, Ji-moo Park sank a forty-footer for birdie on the last hole for a win. The Stanford girl dropped to the ground and cursed.

Next, after Cecile Bisson and her foe slopped around in the rough like choking dogs, the French girl sank a fifteen-foot par putt to topple another Stanford girl, who snapped her own putter over her knee and hurled it into a bunker.

Then Heidi Jung redeemed herself. Just when things looked hopeless for the Cheetahs, she hit a super second shot off a difficult sidehill lie and dropped a curling twenty-foot birdie putt to clinch the national championship.

The Stanford girl's head drooped, she put her hands on her knees, held that position for a moment, then stood up and hollered, "Western Ohio? I don't even know where that IS!"

Our girls hugged on each other. Glenda and Charlie hugged. Glenda and Rita Jo hugged. Everybody lifted up Heidi Jung and tossed her around for sinking the winning putt. Some of the other coaches, a mixture of men and women, came around to congratulate Glenda. So did three ADs who were present. Rita Jo didn't know one of them, but he introduced himself. He was Bud Garrett, new in the job at Maryland. The Terps had finished last in the tournament.

Glenda and Bud Garrett hit it off immediately. He let her know they had the same ocean in common. He was from Wrightsville Beach, born and raised. He knew where Flat Beach was. He'd been the AD at the University of North Carolina–Wilmington when Maryland hired him. It was a challenge moving into the Big 10, but it was a step up in his career.

Goodbyes were said.

Rita Jo was heading back to O'Hare and a flight home. Glenda announced that she and Charlie and the team were staying another night in Chicago to celebrate. Glenda would turn the girls loose on the town. She had reserved a table at The Pump Room for herself and Charlie.

Bud Garrett said, "The Pump Room? I like your style."

Glenda replied with a smile, "You're welcome to join us."

He said, "Really? I would love to."

Rita Jo noted a frown on Charlie Stall.

* * *

IN THE days and weeks that followed, Glenda became someone I wasn't sure I recognized.

The chancellor threw a big party for her at Bent Oak. The coaches of our other sports teams attended, as did members of the board. Hobo Atkins flew in for the occasion from Italy where he was trying to buy the Roman Forum and move it to downtown Shackayooka.

The highlight of the evening for me was when Janice Clapper and Rochelle Stoddard acted like Glenda was their oldest and dearest friend. To my surprise, Glenda went along with it.

My wife became much in demand as a breakfast and luncheon speaker. She spoke to gatherings of the Rotary Internationals, the Kiwanis Internationals, the Optimist Internationals, the Lions Club, the Cheetah Club, the League of Women Voters, and the National Rifle Association.

While all that was going on, she was busy designing the national championship ring for her golf girls—and herself. The ring wound up consisting of a big orange gemstone set in gold and circled by small diamonds.

There were moments when I thought Glenda was becoming a trifle arrogant, but there were other moments when I enjoyed watching her take her victory laps.

THIRTY EIGHT

THE HOUR of decision involving my future finally arrived. It was close to five o'clock and I was fixing my first potato vodka martini of the day when the call came from Eddie Ralph Stoddard, lawyer to rich people only. Eddie Ralph said the board members were unanimous in their vote on how wealthy they were going to make me. He said Roy Clapper and Chancellor Warren Carpenter were on their way over to my office to present the plan to me in person, and they'd invited him to come along.

I said, "Am I gonna be happy?"

Eddie Ralph said, "Now, Pete . . ."

I said, "More importantly, is Glenda gonna be happy?"

He said, "Is she ever—without a golf club in her hand?"

I said, "Let me think about that one."

Eddie Ralph said, "The offer seems generous to me, Pete, but I don't know what you're expecting. Anyhow, I'd rather you hear it from Roy."

I said, "Eddie, if being a mole was your full-time job, you'd be living in a night shelter."

He said, "I'm giving you a heads up, aren't I? See you in a jiffy."

I'd finished bringing out the ice bucket and glasses, and every brand of whiskey I had in stock, and arranging chairs, when Roy and the chancellor and Eddie Ralph entered my office. They were all smiles.

The chancellor came over to give me a fist bump, after which he followed Roy and Eddie Ralph to the bar. They made their own cocktails, doctoring them with care. With drinks in their hands, they moseyed around my office studying the memorabilia and photos on the walls to see if there was anything new that deserved a comment.

I moseyed with them, wondering how long they were going to keep me in suspense. Were they going to make me plush in my sunset years, or farm me out to an assisted living community?

They paused to look at the photo of Kenny "Golden Kid" Sealy striking the Heisman pose after wriggling free from an Iowa Hawkeye.

Eddie Ralph said, "Kenny Sealy sure was fun to watch. How 'bout that sixty-nine-yard run against Indiana? He must have changed directions five times before he was chased out of bounds on the Indiana sideline. Even the Indiana coach gave him a high-five."

Roy Clapper said, "None of us will forget Kenny in the Sugar Bowl. What he did to Auburn, man. Brought us back from eighteen points down in the second half. I'm not sure the law allows you to have more than one Kenny Sealy in a lifetime."

Chancellor Carpenter said, "I pray for another one every Sunday."

I said, "The law better allow it if we want to keep winning. Coach Tag says if you don't have a quarterback today who can throw *and* run, you can give your soul to God because your ass belongs to Ohio State."

Roy said, "How's Omar Mustafa doing in the pros? He was Kenny's go-to guy. You never hear much about him."

I said, "That's because he plays for the Seahawks. Seattle is a little out of the loop. Four of five time zones from most of America's press deadlines, not to mention the country itself. He's doing okay, actually. He's their leading pass receiver. But you wouldn't be aware of this unless you know your way around a computer."

Eddie Ralph said, "I did read somewhere that he's changed his name back to Johnny Gates."

I said, "Yeah, he did. After the draft. He blamed the Muslim name he'd given himself for no NFL team drafting him until the fifth round. He said to Coach Tag, 'That Muslim thing might have worked for Ali and Jabbar, but it didn't do squat for me.'"

The chancellor said, "I'm pleased to hear he changed his name back. It speaks well for the education our university gave him."

Roy said, "Hear, hear."

Looking at the wall again, Eddie Ralph said, "What's this thug doing up here, Pete?"

He was staring at the photo of Adidas Nike Smith completing his trademark rotorhead, disposal, whoa-daddy dunk.

I said, "It's a great photo . . . and he wasn't a thug when he was here fillin' it for us."

The chancellor said, "Here's old Farm Dog."

He stood in front of the posed-action photo of Riley Holt charging at the camera, looking eager to have a head-on with a Ram pickup.

"Riley is the finest linebacker I'll ever see," I said. "There'll be a gross of ACLs in the National Football League before he's done at Green Bay."

Eddie Ralph, still perusing my walls, said, "Wow! The Big Three. Pete Wallace, Rita Jo Foster, and Hobo Atkins."

I said, "We were presenting Hobo the Big Cat 'O Fame Award."

Roy Clapper said, "I don't have that one. How come I've never received that award?"

I said, "Sorry, Roy. I thought you had. I'll get Rita Jo on it."

The chancellor said, "You have to admit Hobo took us on a great trip to New York City."

◼ ◼ ◼

HOBO HAD wanted to show off his new private jet, the Global 5000. It accommodated eleven of us comfortably. The group included Hobo and his wife Melody, who texted her way there and back, Glenda and me, Roy and Janice, Rita Jo and Eddie Ralph, whose wife Rochelle was too busy with her local volunteer work to come along, and Chancellor Carpenter, who brought his secretary—and mistress—Dolores Winters. His wife Bernice refuses to fly.

Bernice says earthbound people are not meant to float around in the air. Things that go up in the air have to come back down—it's a matter of science—and often they come down with a splat. She understood that private jets were said to be the safest way to travel, but she said they crashed all the time, only you never hear about it unless there's a movie star on board.

The Global 5000 avoided every bump in the sky round-trip, and we enjoyed snacks and drinks while we listened to Hobo tell us about the dozens of people he had outwitted in business. Everyone stayed in the Plaza Hotel as a guest of Hobo. The price for Hobo's generosity was having to join him for dinner the first night in the hotel's Oak Room Bar and hear about two of his future business plans.

One plan was to buy Grant's Tomb on New York City's Riverside Drive and move it to a prominent spot on our campus where people can stand and study it instead of driving past it like they were coming out of Turn Two at Indy. Grant was a native son of Ohio and deserved better attention.

Hobo confessed he was facing roadblocks in an effort to close the deal. "Some people are just stubborn," he said.

Another project was to buy Staten Island, relieving New York City of its fifth borough, which the city didn't care about anyhow. He would turn it into one of his residences with a yacht club and game preserve. It would mean relocating over 400,000 people, but they would be happier living in New Jersey, where most of them worked. He would have to demolish the three bridges connecting New Jersey to his newest home. Why make things easy for terrorists?

We were free the second day. Rita Jo and Eddie Ralph and I went to see the Pin Stripes play the Red Sox at Yankee Stadium. It wasn't the Yankee Stadium of Babe Ruth and Lou Gehrig, but it was still Yankee Stadium. I ate four hotdogs with sauerkraut and mustard.

Glenda wanted to play a famous golf course. Hobo showed off by taking her in a limo to Winged Foot in Westchester County. He wasn't a member but he somehow got them on the course. Glenda shot a 78 from the up-front tees with six three-putts. She came back to tell me that Winged Foot's greens would make a good addition to Disney World. Hobo hit very few golf shots on the front nine, then quit on the back. But he rode along in the cart, firing people on his cell.

Before they went to play golf, Hobo had sent Melody to Bergdorf Goodman to buy clothes and have beauty work done.

Janice Clapper made Roy take the boat trip around Manhattan. She returned to say that everybody on board was somebody you never wanted to see again. Dolores Winters had never been to

New York. The chancellor said he'd give her the grand tour. They started with lunch at 21 but stayed the rest of the day, through cocktail hour, dinner, and closing.

I said, "Hobo Atkins is something else. I try not to think about the possibility of him being led away in cuffs someday."

Roy moved to the group photo of our girl golfers who'd won the national championship. Tapping on the glass with his index finger, he said: "This is a pretty girl here on the end. Healthy upstairs, too."

I said, "That's Marta Nystrom. She's Swedish."

Roy said, "I wonder how she gets her swing around those?"

I said, "I'm sure there's an instruction book somewhere that explains it."

Roy took a chair across from my desk. The chancellor and Eddie Ralph followed, taking seats next to Roy. I went to my swivel chair.

Roy Clapper said, "Pete, I'll cut to the chase. We want you to stay on as our athletic director for three more years, and we're here to money-whip you into doing it."

"You're shitting me."

That's the only thing I could think of to say when I could speak. It was the last thing I'd expected to hear from them.

Roy said, "Pete, you've been the best thing that ever happened to Western Ohio University. Your leadership has put us on the national scene in the sports world, and it's paid off for us in more ways than financially."

I said, "Roy, I've been making retirement plans for the last six months. Do you know how tired I am? Most ADs don't stay around half as long as I have."

Roy said, "We're here to make you a little less tired, Pete. They say the sixties are the new forties, anyhow. Haven't you heard?"

I said, "Yeah, I keep hearing that, but I've never heard it from a sumbitch in his sixties."

Roy said, "Lay it out for him, Warren."

The chancellor said, "The board didn't spend much time on this. They wanted to show their appreciation for what you've done here. They voted to bump you up from eight-fifty to a million two immediately."

I said, "That's nice, but . . ."

The chancellor said, "I'm just getting started, Pete. The second year we'll increase your salary to two million."

I said, "My goodness, guys."

The chancellor said, "We're not done. The third year your salary will go up again to two million five. And there'll be bonuses."

He rattled off the bonuses. One hundred thousand for a conference championship in any sport, men's or women's. Two hundred thousand for a national championship in any minor sport, men's or women's. And half a million for a national championship in football or basketball.

I said, "You guys know how to make a man sleep better."

Roy said, "Don't let your chest swell up too big, Pete. Coach Taggert will still be making three times as much as you . . . fucking football coaches."

I said, "You're offering me more zeroes than I ever thought I'd see in one lifetime. What's in the fine print, Roy? There must be something."

Roy said, "There is. You'll be in charge of getting us a new football stadium built—with all the bells and whistles on it."

I said, "We'd have to tear down this one and start from scratch if you want to do it right."

Roy said, "We understand. We want a 60,000-seat bowl with luxury suites, preferred boxes, private clubs, modern concessions, well-spaced restrooms, escalators, elevators, and a Hall of Fame rotunda to honor our past. We might have to buy up more land for parking. We're already a little cramped."

The chancellor said, "It's no hill for you to climb, Pete. You've proved to us that you're up to any challenge. You build this stadium for us, hell, we'll name it after you."

Roy said, "We'll do exactly that. We'll engrave your name in big letters on the West Side façade. Screw Cootie Walters. He's dead anyway."

I said, "I hope you know the stadium you want could cost up to five hundred million. More if you want a retractable roof."

Roy said, "We want a modern stadium, but we don't want a roof. Weather is part of the tradition of Big 10 football. Michigan's stadium holds 107,000 and Ohio State's stadium holds 105,000. Neither one has a roof, but you couldn't get a ticket to any of their home games without mugging somebody."

I said, "No roof, good. It'll make it easier to sell luxury suites. Rich folks don't like inclement weather. Buying a suite will make them feel like they're helping build the stadium . . . and they'll like keeping dry and warm while they entertain friends with food and drink and watch a snow bowl or a mud bath. I'm sure you'll want one, Roy. You too, Eddie Ralph. I guess the chancellor's suite will come free. One of his perks."

The chancellor said, "I certainly hope so. We'll help you in whatever way we can, Pete. Keep in mind that we have friends and alums all over the country—in banks, investment houses, insurance, real estate, energy. There are people we can lean on."

Roy said, "In foreign countries, too."

I said, "I didn't know America had any foreign friends left."

Roy said, "We don't if you're talking about politics. I'm talking about finance. The real world."

I said, "I knew I should have paid more attention in business class when I was in college."

Roy said, "Everything's a matter of economics, Pete."

I said, "I have another question, Roy. Am I gonna like what my financial package will look like when I *do* retire?"

Roy said, "I personally guarantee it. May I take it you're accepting our offer?"

I said, "You don't have to strike a match on my dick. You got me."

Roy said, "All right!"

Roy and the chancellor exchanged high-fives. Roy and Eddie Ralph exchanged high-fives. The chancellor and Eddie Ralph exchanged high-fives. Then they each gave me a high-five.

I said, "I don't know how Glenda is going to take this. She's been counting on us moving away and buying homes in far-off lands where she can play golf year-round."

Roy said, "Where you'll be bored to death."

I said, "Maybe not. I've sort of been looking forward to my leisure years."

Eddie Ralph said, "I didn't know you liked to paint, Pete."

I laughed.

He said, "You might get lucky and live close to a bingo parlor."

I said to Roy, "Before I sign anything—and before you get run over by a truck—I want it in writing about my future retirement package when I do go."

Roy said, "Not to worry. You shall have it."

I said, "And I want Rita Jo taken care of in this new deal."

Roy said, "You name it. Whatever it is, she'll damn sure be worth it."

I said, "It'll be sizable. I don't want to lose her."

Roy looked at me with a twinkle, and said, "I don't see much danger of that, Pete."

THIRTY NINE

WHEN THE brass left my office, I sat in a comfortable silence for a while, sipping a freshened martini and seeing so many dollar signs and zeroes hovering around the ceiling I thought I might need to visit my retina guy.

I decided that Glenda deserved to hear from me first before Rita Jo. Plus I wanted to get that conversation out of the way, not knowing whether to take the over or the under on how unhappy Glenda was gonna be when she heard I'd re-upped for three more years. She didn't answer her cell. She didn't answer the home phone. Nobody at Bent Oak could find her, not even Charlie Stall, and I had him look everywhere—the practice range, putting green, mixed grill, pro shop. I even tried the Town Club.

It was unlike my wife to be completely out of touch.

Then the mystery was solved.

It was solved when a guy from a messenger service poked his head in my office to deliver me a letter. It was from Glenda.

With surprise, astonishment, and a lump of mixed feelings, I read:

Pete:

This is to let you know I have filed for divorce and I will be moving across the country. It is something I should have done before now. Our marriage has never been anything more than an experiment that never really worked. But I didn't have the will or the gumption or a glimpse at a brighter future to do anything about it.

Now I do.

It's easy enough to obtain a no-fault divorce these days, but I still had to come up with a plea. I flipped a coin between incompatibility and irreconcilable differences, and incompatible won.

I have accepted the job as the women's golf coach at the University of Maryland. As you know, after my girls won the NCAA I've received offers from several schools— Florida State, Missouri, Iowa State, and Maryland among them—and I know I have made the right choice.

Maryland has its own university golf course—a pretty good one—and that will be a helpful recruiting tool for me. I plan to work my heart out turning the Maryland Terps into the best women's golf program in the country.

It was a wonderful feeling to be in demand. Something I had never known before. If you want to accuse me of giving up life for golf, you may be right.

I've made a down payment on a little waterfront place in Oxford, Maryland, a small but picturesque town on a river that feeds into Chesapeake Bay. Not exactly a fast commute to the College Park campus, but it will be worth it to be back living near the ocean where I was raised.

Pete, there is no reason why this split should cause a financial quarrel. I have been informed that Ohio is a marital property state. This means that everything we have accumulated during our marriage must be divided down the middle. Possessions, savings, stocks, investments, and so forth. I am happy with that. Can we avoid a war between costly lawyers?

You will find that I have taken part of my wardrobe with me along with some of my golf clubs and Marissa and Clive. I will arrange for the rest of my things to be moved as soon as possible.

I know you will miss the doggies, but I would miss them more.

I hope the board did right by you in your retirement compensation today, but I'm betting they low-balled you as usual.

I wish you well, Pete. Let's try to remember that we did have some good times. Just not as many as we both would have wanted.

Glenda

▣ ▣ ▣

I READ the letter again, and read it one more time, and nothing changed in it. I kept having the same reaction. What the hell is this? Are you kidding me? Jesus, she's serious. She's gone.

I was shocked. Stuff swirled around in my head. One thing kept speaking to me. I'd lived with a woman for over twenty years but never really knew her.

Sad deal.

Needless to say, I had a lot to think about.

So I sipped my martini, chewed on an olive—and thought.

FORTY

RITA JO let out a whoop through the phone when I told her the board had money-whipped me into staying around for three more years. But before I could tell her anything else, she hung up after saying, "Break out the white wine—I'll be there in ten minutes."

It seemed like she arrived faster than that. I heard her coming and stood up and walked around my desk to greet her.

She bounded into my office in a pair of black leggings, a baggy gray sweatshirt, her hair in a white headband, and leaped into my arms and landed a juicy kiss on me.

Recovering, I said, "Is that all you think about my decision to re-up?"

She said, "You want to know the best thing about it?"

I said, "I would, yes."

She said, "It gives me three more years to try to break up your less-than-ideal marriage."

I said, "Then you might find this interesting." I handed her Glenda's letter.

She said, "What is it?"

"Read it," I said.

Rita Jo took a chair. I poured her a glass of white wine, and sat back behind my desk to study her reaction as she read the letter.

Her eyes widened as she read the first sentence, then looked up at me.

I said, "Yes . . . ?"

She said, "As a communications graduate from this university, I can tell you this much right off the bat: She didn't bury the lead."

I said, "Nope. She didn't."

She read the rest of the letter calmly.

When she finished, she placed the letter on an end table, sipped her wine, looked at me, and said, "I wish I still smoked."

I grinned.

She said with a serious look, "How do you feel about this?"

I said, "I didn't see it coming. Maybe I should have. Can a man feel a little sad, a little guilty, and a little relieved—all at the same time?"

She said, "It's in the rulebook."

With that, she slowly stood up and came around and pulled me out of my chair and put her arms around my neck.

She laid another kiss on me. It wasn't sisterly. I helped out.

She said, "Pete, I've been in love with you forever . . . and I know you've been in love with me for almost ever. I'm sure of this. How did we keep from tempting fate all this time?"

I said, "You were a kid when I hired you. We became close friends and worked together. I didn't want to risk spoiling a great friendship."

She said with a sparkle, "But how could you resist me?"

I said, "I'm not sure. I guess I just relied on character and integrity."

She laughed.

We held hands.

She said, "So, knowing what we now know, what do you see in the future for us?"

I said, "Well . . . if you're talking about life and love and stuff, I can only share with you the words of a wise old philosopher I once knew."

Giggling, she said, "Whose words were . . . ?"

I pulled her close, and said, "Whatever happen, happen."

OTHER BOOKS BY DAN JENKINS

NOVELS

The Franchise Babe
Slim and None
The Money-Whipped Steer-Job Three-Jack Give-Up Artist
You Gotta Play Hurt
Rude Behavior
Fast Copy
Life Its Ownself
Baja Oklahoma
Limo (with Bud Shrake)
Dead Solid Perfect
Semi-Tough

NONFICTION

Unplayable Lies
His Ownself: A Semi-Memoir
Jenkins at the Majors
Fairways and Greens
I'll Tell You One Thing
Bubba Talks
You Call It Sports But I Say It's a Jungle Out There
Saturday's America
The Dogged Victims of Inexorable Fate
The Best 18 Golf Holes in America